# RICHARD
# LAMB

Center Point
Large Print

Also by Richard S. Wheeler and available from Center Point Large Print:

*The Two Medicine River*

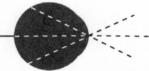

**This Large Print Book carries the
Seal of Approval of N.A.V.H.**

# RICHARD LAMB

# Richard S. Wheeler

CENTER POINT LARGE PRINT
THORNDIKE, MAINE

This Center Point Large Print edition is published
in the year 2014 by arrangement with
Golden West Literary Agency.

The text of this Large Print edition is unabridged.
In other aspects, this book may vary from the original edition.
Printed in the United States of America on permanent paper.
Set in 16-point Times New Roman type.

ISBN: 978-1-62899-348-6 (hardcover)
ISBN: 978-1-62899-355-4 (paperback)


Library of Congress Cataloging-in-Publication Data

Wheeler, Richard S.
Richard Lamb / Richard S. Wheeler. —
   Center Point Large Print edition.
pages ; cm
Summary: "Richard Lamb was a peace-loving man hoping to live out
the rest of his days with his Indian wife and their large extended family,
but the Partridge brothers had other plans—deadly plans to advance
their careers. All they needed was a little Indian resistance"—Provided
by publisher.
ISBN 978-1-62899-348-6 (hardcover : alk. paper) —
ISBN 978-1-62899-355-4 (pbk. : alk. paper)
1. Indians of North America—Fiction.  2. Large type books.  I. Title.
PS3573.H4345R5 2014
813'.54—dc23
                                                    2014028584

For Loren D. Estleman

# CHAPTER 1

Like Job, Richard Lamb was content to live out his old age surrounded by the things he loved. In the predawn gray, he stretched beneath his fine albino buffalo robe, feeling the inert warmth of his wife beside him, then rose to meet the sun.

It was a thing he always did, this greeting of the newborn sun. Now, in June, he rose very early, but in the winter he slept long. The sky was cloudless and this fine day promised to be like the day before, and like a thousand others.

He was seventy-seven, having been born an hour into the new century, on January 1, 1800. In his prime he had been tall and lean; now he was still lean, but age had shrunk him. He made a point of standing straight because he despised the stooped posture of the old. He wore a great white beard shot with gunmetal black hairs and kept neatly trimmed. His hairline had receded halfway back upon his scalp and what hair he had left hung shoulder length, the way of the mountain men. One piercing azure eye, sunk into blistered, crevassed, umber flesh, gazed out upon creation. Over the other eye was a blackened leather patch, held in place by a band.

With his good eye Richard Lamb studied the familiar meadows from the high verandah of his

7

massive log home. Like all good days, this one was born in silence. There was mist upon the creek and no breeze stirred the cottonwoods. Across empty distances to the east lay rolling plains, now obscured in the dawn gloom. To the northeast lay the Snowy Mountains, the towering eastern sentinels of the Rockies, standing in splendid isolation above the high northern plains. Richard Lamb could not see the mountains from where he stood, but he knew they were there. To the northwest lay Coffin Butte, a well-named giant. But it was the prospect to the south and west that always stirred the old man's heart.

From his home amid the cottonwoods along Elk Creek rose layer upon layer of tumbling green foothills that gave way to black forest and then to the towering white northern massif of the Crazy Mountains. For fifty years his eyes had recorded that panorama and his soul had always been stirred by it.

Perhaps there were grander views in the northern Rockies, but he did not know them. Always his thoughts returned to this place in the drainage of the Upper Musselshell, and whenever he could spare time from trapping he came here to where the high plains—the buffalo land—shouldered the craggiest of the mountains in the whole territory of Montana.

The old man stretched in his long johns, watching the low sun blazon the Crazies, watching the plains shimmer in the dawn, watching the young leaves of the noble cotton-woods stir in the softest of zephyrs.

He had chosen this place purely for aesthetic reasons, with none of the hard calculation of an experienced rancher who studies soils and grasses and water and shelter and distances to markets. No, Richard Lamb was a man in love with a place. He had come and settled long before, in 1850. Then he had smiled at Mother Nature and had said, This is the most beautiful place in the world, and it sets my soul to soaring; and Mother Nature, more used to being raped than smiled at, had replied, Raise your cattle here, and your sheep, and take good care of my earth, and your life will go well.

It had been a good life. He had been reared in Amherst in the Commonwealth of Massachusetts, the only son of Horace Lamb, a proper professor of classics and rhetoric, and his wife Matilda. In the quiet, green-canopied village of Amherst, Richard had learned his classics well and ancient history too, before attending Harvard College over at Cambridge. Then as a youthful assistant professor, he had returned to his father's campus to teach, whiling away his springtime pleasantly in the bosom of Academe—until he grew bored with words and paper and an old man's life. He knew there were better things. A vast wilderness, for example.

After spring term he had quietly packed, said goodbye to his startled parents, and headed west toward St. Louis—and never looked back. He had joined the Ashley expedition and toiled his way into a stunning new life.

He was young and he was free.

He had first seen this place in the autumn of 1831 when he, in a small company led by Jim Bridger, had trapped Elk Creek for a while. It was a dangerous place to be, well within the southern reaches of Blackfeet lands. Along the lower creek was ample evidence that it was a favorite summer ground of Bug's Boys. There were firepits, middens of bones, abandoned lodgepoles, and dried horse dung dotting the lush meadows up and down the creek.

But this was not a good wintering place, since the whole land opened out upon the north, naked before the arctic winds. And so the Piegans or Siksika who summered here left for more sheltered places. Richard Lamb learned to come here in the spring and the fall and gaze upon this Eden where he would some day build his home. He never failed, through all the years of trapping beaver, to visit this sacred place and dream his dreams.

By 1840 the fur trade had declined, and Richard Lamb eked out a small living from trapping and trading buffalo hides, needing little more than powder and galena for his Hawken, and a few supplies. It was still dangerous to come here alone, and not until smallpox devastated the Blackfeet federation was it possible to linger beneath these giant cottonwoods beside the laughing creek.

In 1850 he settled at last, already a graying middle-aged man. And by then he was not alone. His young Siksika wife, Aspen, and their twin five-year-old daughters were with him. There upon the dancing creek he had slowly erected a great, solid, log home—he and those brothers of Aspen he could employ, such as Black Wolf. It was to be both a home and a trading post. For fine peltries and good buffalo robes he would trade knives and muskets and lead and powder and cast-iron pots and iron arrowheads and calico and four-point blankets and a lot more, freighted up by river packet to Fort Benton on the Missouri. On one of those packets came a bull and bred cow, and sheep and chickens and apple saplings, all of which he had carefully nourished into herds and flocks and orchards until he was able in the 1860s to supply the mining camps of Helena and Bannock and Virginia City and Confederate Gulch and Maiden and Butte with beef and lamb and eggs and fruit.

The girls grew; in 1861 he married them off to fine Siksika youths, and now there were seven Blackfeet lodges up the creek a bit, with an army of relatives the old man could hardly keep straight—especially the grandchildren—and all of them helping him run a large enterprise and enjoy the peace and security of his fortress home. No tribe had ever attacked it, for word of his fair dealing had spread east to the Sioux and Cheyenne and south to the Crow and west to the Flathead and Shoshone. But even though it was manned by Blackfeet, it was a neutral post and frequently was visited by Indians for whom the word Siksika had meant mortal enemy for as long as the elders could remember.

As the old man gazed out upon the great massif of the Crazy Mountains, still white this June day and glowing pinkly in the long sun, he thanked God—as he always did—for this day and this place. For although he had discarded the whole of white civilization, he retained a firm and wondrous sense of God, of a Lord of this Creation that had permitted him to live so well and so long and in such fine health among those he loved. His focus dropped to the seven lodges two hundred yards away. Smoke from breakfast fires curled up from some of them.

One lodge belonged to his daughter Hope, also called Tall Grass Bending, and her husband Turtle. Another to Faith, or Spring Willow, and her husband Standing Bear. These and three other lodges were of buffalo cowhide, darkened by smoke to a fine chestnut that deepened to black near the upper smokehole and windflaps. Two of the lodges, those of the younger kin, were of canvas duck and gleamed whitely in the dawn haze. Buffalo were scarce now and the hide lodges could no longer be made or even repaired; the canvas duck sheeting, sewn by some entrepreneur in far-off Minnesota, had become a prized trade item among the northern tribes. The canvas was lighter, stronger, and easier to handle, but colder too and less able to resist the hard rain than a fine smoke-soaked buffalo cowhide lodge.

That spring, realizing that the buffalo were nearly gone, the old man had instructed his clan to drive as many of the great black beasts as they could gather into an obscure canyon in the foothills of the Crazies to hide them from the plague of hidehunters who had almost destroyed the northern herd and were now wiping out the last of the southern. These sacred buffalo his clan had hidden in a wild land, and now a young herder was always in attendance to steer the shaggy giants away from the eyes of whites. There were a hundred or so, and care was taken to slaughter very few—only the decrepit, if possible.

Today, as on all other days, his in-laws and children and grandchildren and sons-in-law and their parents would drift into the foothills to watch over the cattle and sheep, as well as the buffalo. Still others would watch the horse band and protect it from their ancient enemies, the Crow. The women would tend the gardens and keep the lodges. One or two of the young, expert with the single-shot rifles Lamb had given them, would ride off to the high country and bring back an elk or white-tailed deer, or perhaps a mountain ram.

I am rich, thought the old man. For on this day, once again, the sun will make the great high prairie shimmer and the clean sweet air will eddy about these old bones with a dry comfort unknown in the sweaty east. And I will have my loved ones gathered around me and see the grandchildren grow and my daughters and their families prosper.

"Your face shines," said Aspen. She stood beside him in the June dawn, tall and angular, still young. The Blackfeet are a tall people.

"I have ye," he replied.

"And all this."

"This too," he said, smiling.

"But all things are taken away."

"Yes, eventually."

"What is this word, 'eventually'?" asked his wife.

"In time. Something to come."

"Maybe soon," she said. She slipped inside and Richard Lamb heard her in the kitchen making the noises of cooking.

Maybe soon, he agreed. It was a time of war. The great alliance of Sioux and Cheyenne had defeated Custer a year earlier. And now this year was torn by the clash of arms. But here, in this

14

obscure corner of Montana Territory, peace reigned and the warm sun greened the grasses.

He gazed contentedly at the horse herd in the meadows to the east, loving the sight of them almost as much as he loved the great prospect of the Crazy Mountains. Even now, a teenage grandson, Luke Old Coyote, was out among them. He was not merely herding the horses, but handling and training them as well.

Five were Lamb's own. One dun mustang was a pensioner like himself, the son of another dun mustang he had ridden when he first came to settle here. Another was an off-white stallion, a tall animal with black spots on his rump—a medicine horse that invested its owner with great power in war and was itself invulnerable to arrow or bullet or lance. It was of a kind raised by the Nez Percé to the west, a tribe now being hounded off its farmlands by the army. Two others were sorrels, and the fifth was a young bay that Luke had begun to gentle. They looked fat and sleek in the sun, and most of their winter hair was gone.

There were about twenty other horses, some colts but most of them rideable or broke to harness, and all of them a temptation to their horse-stealing neighbors.

Up the creek, where the lodges stood, his bronzed kin were performing their ablutions at the creek. Most Blackfeet bathed daily, the men and women in separate places, and waded into the creeks and streams in even bitterly cold weather when white men would cringe. Now he saw them distantly, naked in the snow-melt creek.

He stretched stiffly, not feeling his age but aware of it all the time now, and reentered his log home through massive doors. The room he entered was his trading post. Behind a thick pine counter were shelves of goods: bolts of bright calico, trading blankets, traps, pots, pans, iron arrow tips, knives, beads, barrels of sugar and flour and coffee beans and molasses, and more. The rifles and shot and cartridges were in a locked cabinet.

Here traders came off the plains, in whole bands or singly, to offer fine buffalo robes or beaver pelts or otter skins or doe skins or elk hides. Richard Lamb traded, gave fair measure, never cheated, and made a small profit. A greater part of his income came from feeding the mining camps. But the trading protected his home. There was always, among the plains tribes, a respected neutrality surrounding the trading posts. Mortal enemies, Crow and Siksika, would camp in a trading post's shadow without harm, even though two or three miles away, they would cheerfully murder each other. Richard Lamb also liked the fact that the post brought friends, and he prized above all his hundreds of Indian friends.

Still, as the old mountain man knew, there was no substitute out here, an infinity from help, for a strong and defensible place. The great post was a fortress. The roof of peeled lodgepole lay under two feet of fireproof sod. There were loopholes in the walls and heavy shutters for the high windows. Water, food, and arms were all stored against siege.

The trading room across the front of the building was also its parlor. Behind it were a kitchen and two small bedrooms. The one that had housed the girls was now an office and the home of a few precious books the old man treasured. It was a place Aspen rarely entered. She was afraid of this place, with the talking books and white man's mysteries.

Richard Lamb padded to the bedroom and pulled on fine fringed buckskin trousers and a buckskin shirt over his long johns. In earlier years there would have been no long-handled under-wear, but age had taken the fire out of his body and an old man could feel as chilled in June as in January. The buckskins were tanned to a golden cream and did not at all resemble the grease and smoke-blackened skins he wore in younger years as a trapper. Upon these shining light skins were beading and quillwork in riotous colors and sacred designs, the loving labor of Aspen's long winter days. And so he was dressed as richly as Blackfeet art could dress him when he stepped into the kitchen, a tall, erect, bearded patriarch. He smiled. Aspen was dressed in equally exquisite skirts. She was tall and angular, and as striking as the day he had married her thirty-two years earlier after paying her father, Singing Bird, five fine ponies, two Hudson Bay blankets, one used Hawken, powder and ball, and a promise to beat fair Aspen regularly. Singing Bird had smiled, knowing the soft ways of white-eyes with their women. Richard Lamb thought that if he should lose his other eye and the sight of Aspen, he would lose life itself, for she was more beautiful than the great wall of the Crazies to the south, or the cottonwoods along Elk Creek, or his medicine horse, Wind Rising.

Aspen glanced out the high west window as the old man spooned up his oat gruel and some eggs. "Bigtooth Beaver runs down the Sentinel Hill," she said absently.

He paused. Sentinel Hill, a high foothill ridge that commanded the whole country, was the lookout post. One or another of the youths was always there from dawn to dusk. From that high outpost the keen observer could see a dozen miles in any direction and could report the approach of visitors a full hour or so before their arrival. It was a worthwhile precaution not only for their safety, but to prepare feasts and organize trade goods. And in some cases, to spirit one guest away in a direction opposite that from which another was coming.

The old man frowned. Bigtooth Beaver whipped

his small pinto into a downhill lope—a hard and reckless thing to do—past the lodges, across the creek, and reined sharply at the rear door of the great post.

"Ye risked that pony," said the old man gently, but with an edge.

The chunky golden-skinned boy leapt down and stood apologetically. "I am sorry, Grandfather, there are visitors coming."

Richard Lamb nodded.

"I think they are the bluebelly soldiers, Grandfather."

Lamb frowned. "Why do ye think that, Bigtooth Beaver?"

"They come two by two in a column like a snake, and the man in front has a sword that shines."

"How many?"

"Not many. I think the fingers of my hands would number them."

The old man did not like it. Soldiers were not good news.

"Let the people of the lodges know, Grandson, and let them be ready. And then return to ye'r post."

The youth whirled away on his pony.

I've had many peaceful years, thought Lamb, but now I fear the idyll has ended.

# CHAPTER 2

Peter Partridge was getting his first taste of the Great American Desert and already he had summed it up in a single word: forgettable. It was an empty place, fit only for the savages that inhabited it. One desolate range of mountains after another, rising from tongues of high prairie with nothing upon it at all—no sign even of animal life. Still, there were stories here and he had come west for stories.

Young Peter Partridge was a correspondent for the *New York Herald* and had made his reluctant way west to cover the Indian wars. Long miles on gritty railroads and then an eternity on a Missouri River packet that had, ultimately, deposited him at Fort Benton, Montana Territory. He had sent dispatches back regularly: descriptions of the sights and sounds of the frontier and its rude denizens.

He was, he knew, a good writer, with a keen eye for the unusual and a gift for drawing out the taciturn. He asked questions and generated fine stories. But the question for which there was no answer continued to absorb him: Why did the armed might of the United States pursue savages in this endless wasteland at all? Surely it was no place where civilized men would ever settle and establish banks and clubs and theaters.

He rode easily in the McClellan saddle supplied by his brother, Captain Joseph Partridge. Back east, he had ridden much in Central Park, and into the open country of northern Manhattan, and now was perfectly comfortable on his U.S. Army mount. Those had been pleasant outings—more or less like this, except shorter. He wore, for this occasion, stylish attire, consisting of Harris tweed knickers with fine knee-high argyle stockings and ankle-high kangaroo boots. Over his white shirt (minus his usual celluloid collar) he wore a matching Harris tweed jacket with leather patches at the elbows. At his neck was a fine foulard silk scarf in magenta. In his saddlebags were a sheaf of foolscap and assorted pencils, it being impractical to carry nib pens and ink in these wastes. He was a freckled, sandy man, green-eyed, with muttonchops of caramel-colored hair adorning the cheeks of his moonlike face. This round face was what separated him from his more saturnine but similarly tinted older brother, Joseph, riding beside him.

This wasn't Delmonico's, and the absence of female company was a hardship, but Peter Partridge was cheery nonetheless. In New York he would not have worn the Colt's .45 revolver holstered beneath his jacket. This, too, he knew how to use with deadly accuracy, having belonged to a New York rod and gun society for years. He had assiduously cultivated all the manly arts, on the supposition that they would be useful during his roving.

Among the mysteries he hoped to plumb was just how these ignorant savages in skins would give the U.S. Army, with its modern technology, such a bad time of it. The Custer disaster lay upon the centennial year as a puzzle, and even now, a year later, these nomadic bands seemed to elude and mock the great commanders, such as Gibbon, Terry, Crook, and Howard. Peter suspected that the generals were idiots. When he first beheld these savages—of the Blackfeet species he was told—at Fort Benton, he found nothing formidable or dangerous about them. Indeed, they seemed mostly drunken and degraded.

But plumbing the mysteries of Indian war was not the purpose of Peter Partridge's long journey into the West. He had come to rescue Joseph, although the captain did not know that. It had been their father's idea. At his New York club one recent night, the senior Partridge had laid it out: "Joe's trapped at an obscure post, and his career stymied. Go out there, Peter, and stir the pot. You have a quick, bright mind. Write stories. Better yet, put some ideas in his head or he'll rot at Fort Shaw for a decade. I didn't raise captains—I raised generals."

And now they were on a mission that was rife with possibility. With his clever pen he could even make something of this obscure squad of mounted infantry, riding along an obscure creek that drained into the Upper Musselshell, an obscure river that drained, far away, into the Missouri.

The *New York Herald* would be the instrument of Joe's advancement. All Peter needed, really, was a little trouble, a little resistance, a little war—anything would do—and Joe Partridge would be a hero. There were going to be dispatches under a Publius byline extolling the brave courage and wilderness wisdom of one Joseph Partridge, of Albany, New York. Those dispatches, Peter knew, would suffice to bring official esteem and reward to his brother, and a blocked career would advance once again. That was the way of the Partridges. The brothers were scions of a grand Albany merchant family that understood the ways of the world. When things could not be attained by enterprise or private diligence, they might yet be attained through political maneuver and the creation of public esteem. That, indeed, was how Joseph got his commission as a second lieutenant. But afterward, Joseph had officered commendably on the frontier for over ten years and had risen on merit. Like all Partridges, Joseph was a man to reckon with.

"What do you do for women out here, Joe?" asked the correspondent.

"Why, there are none, save the squaws, so we do nothing. Perhaps you can send me one from New York."

"A dismal way to live. I could not stand it," said Peter.

"The squaws make fine wives if one is inclined in that direction, I hear," said Joseph. "The mountain men took them, sometimes several, and preferred them to whites. Indian marriages are, eh, loose, you know."

"A teepee mate. Not for me. I should like a mistress of a good New York brownstone."

"Well, you'll meet one soon enough—a squaw man, that is. Lamb and his Blackfeet woman, and a collection of breeds. That's where we're going first."

"Another story, I imagine. Tell me about Lamb."

"Nothing to tell. Old man, I hear. Empty life lived as a savage. Runs a trading post and sells beef to the mining camps. All these frontier types—fugitives from civilization—haven't got a brain or an ambition or an education among them."

The captain's eyes, even while addressing his brother beside him, never stopped studying the hills and horizons and the shadowed coulees from which surprises might erupt. Private Grouard was scouting a mile forward and appeared occasionally on a crest. Behind the captain and his civilian brother, pairs of bluecoated infantry, each man armed with a Springfield and a revolver, rode their horses dutifully in column formation. Two pack mules brought up the rear. They had started before June dawn and had covered ten miles from their Musselshell camp.

"We will rest the horses," the captain informed his brother. He raised a gloved hand and the column halted.

"Dismount and water your horses. Johnson and Fiskestand guard. We'll reach Lamb's post in two hours."

They rested in a shallow, naked valley where the creek raced coldly north to the Musselshell. It chilled Peter to be surrounded by nothing. Off to the west rose Coffin Butte, pine-specked in its upper reaches and lit coral by the morning sun.

The two brothers washed and watered, and then idled on a knoll watching the small troop loosen its muscles. Beside them, reined closely, their horses cropped the lush green bunchgrass, which formed saliva-laden lumps around the bits in their mouths.

"How'll that old man take it?" asked Peter.

The captain shrugged. "Hard, I imagine. Those old mountain men don't yield to anything very willingly. They think they're lords of the earth, but they're just refugees and failures, living out beyond the rim of law and society."

"You'll show him the iron fist, eh?"

Joe grinned. "Not unless I have to. . . . He's an old man now."

"But no less barbaric for that. Imagine what a lifetime out here does to character. Primitive, I

25

suppose. Probably just a glorified animal by now, growling and snarling. Take him to New York and put him in the Central Park Zoo."

"Peter, don't underestimate these frontiersmen. Some of those old fellows—Kit Carson, Joseph Walker, Jim Bridger—they taught the United States Army how to exist out here. Fremont would have marched in circles without them. He was the Pathfinder, all right. Found someone else's path, he did."

Peter grinned. "I hope the old boy resists. I can make a better story of it for the *Herald*."

"If he does, you might not live to write about it," Joseph retorted dourly.

Peter fondled the revolver at his waist. "I may be city-bred, but I can hold my own out here."

Joseph grunted rudely. "We don't know how many lodges are there to back him. We could be badly outnumbered."

"Oh come now, Joe. Since when has being outnumbered by savages slowed the U.S. Army?"

"Well—to be precise—June 25, 1876."

Peter slipped into silence. That was a puzzle, that date. He would have liked to interview Colonel Custer before and after that day's events. "Well, Joe," he said at last, "your respect for these lords of the prairie seems exaggerated to me, but I'd rather be in the command of someone as cautious as yourself than in the command of Colonel Custer, who wasn't."

"Time to go," the captain said, rising.

The column formed once again and coiled southward. Peter Partridge, bored by the endless humped prairie, hunkered into himself and began to compose electrifying leads for stories he would dispatch:

June 17, UPPER MUSSELSHELL, Montana Territory: Today a patrol under the command of Captain Joseph Partridge captured a large force of hostiles along with a white man who had reverted to animal savagery, and marched the hostiles north to the Blackfeet reservation. . . .

Dull. A little battle would enliven it, he thought. What sort of story could he find in herding savages like cattle drovers on a trail drive?

"How are you going to do it?" he asked.

"Negotiation."

"And what if they won't negotiate?"

"Force."

"Why not force first? Surround them. Rifles on the hills ready to shoot in. I can make a better story of it. Put you in a better light."

"We are not at war. The Blackfeet are not hostiles. Lamb is a citizen."

"Some citizen! He's never paid a tax in his life, I imagine."

"He's a citizen. So were all those mountain

men, Peter. But for them, the British would possess the northwest territories today."

"How can I make a story—?"

"You can report that I did my job well."

"What are your orders? How much leeway have you?"

"I have some leeway on one item."

"Which is—?"

"I can close the post or not, as I see fit."

"Herding those human cattle to their pens isn't going to earn you a new rank, Joe. You should arrange it so that—"

"Like Custer arranged it. He wanted to be president. I do not want to risk the lives of my enlisted men."

The journalist from New York fell silent. Then he raised a question: "What are your orders, exactly?"

"I have them in my breastpocket but I can recite them well enough. They're from General Terry himself, with supplemental details from Gibbon."

He paused, organizing his memories, his eyes on Grouard who was sitting quietly on a rise half a mile forward. Then he continued, " 'For the duration of the present conflict, remove all Indians, both friendlies and hostiles, to their reservations. Confiscate all arms and ammunition. Orders in effect until further notice, upon con-clusion of hostilities.' That was Terry. Gibbon added, 'Close at discretion any trading post supplying hostiles with arms, or trading in peltries for horses or other implements of war. Confiscate all such arms and relevant materiel at such posts.' "

"You going to close down Lamb?"

"No need. Once we put the Blackfeet and Crow on their reserves, he'll be a hundred fifty miles from them. And the mining camps will still need his beef. There's little enough of it here, with the buffalo about gone."

"If you take his Indians, how's he going to get beef to markets?"

"He can hire white drovers like the rest."

"What if he resists? What if they start shooting?"

"We'll shoot back. But they won't. There's not a one of them that doesn't remember the Baker affair."

"What's that?"

"That's something the army doesn't talk about."

The newsman waited.

"In January of eighteen and seventy," the captain began, "a cavalry command under a Major Baker, out of Fort Ellis down near Bozeman, surrounded a Piegan camp—nonhostile—and then slaughtered nearly the whole of it on the pretext of looking for horse thieves. Something like ninety women, fifty children, and thirty-odd men. Only a few escaped. Shot as they fled their lodges. The camp was undefended. Many were ill with smallpox. A young lieutenant, Pease was his name, I knew him, risked his career to report it. The army was trying to cover it up, and until then no word had reached the East. The report stirred up the Quakers and other bleeding hearts. And the plains Indians. Even though the Blackfeet and Sioux are historic enemies, that slaughter aroused all the northern tribes, and we haven't seen the end of it yet."

"What bearing does that have on this?"

"Blackfeet are frightened to death of soldiers. I'm counting on it."

Peter Partridge grinned.

They were closing now on Private Grouard, who had ridden down from the ridge to the creek trail. The private wheeled his horse and trotted alongside Captain Partridge.

"Cap'n, sir, we've been spotted. Horseman on rise yonder, two miles or so, plunged down slope. Injun from the looks of him. But I couldn't be sure."

"Thank you, Private. We're almost at the post now. You may rejoin the ranks."

He halted the command.

"We are," he announced, "about two miles from Lamb's Post. I'm expecting no trouble but we will be prepared for it. Keep your rifles sheathed. This is a peaceful mission. But be prepared for pistol work at close range if trouble comes.

"When we reach the post, spread out, at least

ten yards between men. Don't bunch up. Any man who shoots without my express command will be in grave trouble with me. We're not at war with these people. All we want to do is escort them north. Remember that.

"We'll start them north fast before they think to complain. They're all nomads, and used to it. If we push them hard, we'll all be back in time for the post ball. Any questions?"

There were none.

They marched two by two through meadows golden with black-eyed Susans swaying warm in the breezes, and out upon a broad flood plain where the creek veered westward through stately cottonwoods in new leaf. And beyond, warm and comfortable under the big sky, lay Lamb's Post in the morning sun, with ice-colored smoke rising from one of its two chimneys.

They rode through the quiet, their Springfields rattling in their sheaths, and their horses' shod hooves crunching upon the coarse gravel, and then drew up in a long line before the post.

There to greet them was a single old man in spotless creamy buckskins decorated riotously with carmine and sky blue beads and dyed quillwork. On his feet were the black moccasins of the Siksika. From behind a great trimmed beard a single azure eye took them in, and casually crooked in his arm was a Henry repeater, polished until it shone.

No Coldstream Guard in shako and redcoat made a grander sight, and no howling bagpipe spoke more of blood and honor than the glistening Henry that seemed so casually pointed at the heart of one, then another, of the troop, before coming to rest, at last—aimed at the heart of Captain Joseph Partridge.

# CHAPTER 3

"Gentlemen?"

That single word sent a shock of recognition through Peter Partridge. That cultivated voice was patrician. He marveled that such a voice could rise from a flamboyantly attired ruffian.

"You are Lamb," said the captain.

"Indeed. And who be ye?"

"Captain Joseph Partridge, commanding a squad from A Company, Fort Shaw. And my brother Peter, who is a reporter for the *New York Herald* and is covering the Indian wars.

"Well, then, ye are welcome. Ye've an eastern voice. Where are ye from, eh?"

"We grew up in Albany, Sir. Peter lives in New York City."

"That's fine. A fine place. What brings ye here?"

"Protection, Mr. Lamb. The United States Army wishes to protect your Blackfeet Indians here from the depredations of the hostiles."

"They are well-protected, thank ye. A trading post is neutral ground, and we are well armed in any case. So we need none, and will make do without."

"I misspoke myself, Sir. I am under orders from Generals Terry and Gibbon to remove all Indians to their reservations."

"I feared as much." The one eye glinted. "And I imagine that's not the whole of it either."

"No, Sir," replied the captain, "it is not. These posts, including yours, are a major source of weapons for the hostiles. I am under orders to confiscate all firearms within, as well as those of your Indians here."

"*All,* Mr. Partridge?"

"Those are my instructions, Sir."

"Mine, for instance? And those of these non-hostile Indians? Our hunting rifles?"

"All, Mr. Lamb."

"There is the matter of the constitution, Sir. Are ye familiar with it? Shall we retire to my study and examine the clause that prohibits the confiscation of private property without just compensation?"

Again Peter marveled. An educated barbarian. Something the man must have absorbed around rude campfires.

Captain Partridge sighed. "If you had wished to live under the protection of the constitution, Mr. Lamb, you would have chosen to live where its writ runs, rather than spending a lifetime beyond the rim of the civilization it regulates. No. The only law here is the law of General Terry. Of course I would be inclined to overlook a hand-gun for your private use. . . ."

"Pray dismount, eh? And perhaps ye and ye'r patrol can enjoy ye'r nooning beneath the cotton-woods yonder. I must explain ye'r mission to my relatives here, and that will take some doing. In fact, it is unexplainable, eh?"

"We will do that, Lamb. But I will place a man within your post there. I'm sure you understand."

Captain Partridge waved Johnson forward. "Stand guard in there, Private. Shoot anyone who attempts to remove firearms or ammunition."

The curly-haired youth dismounted and trudged toward the massive slab door of the post, and tried it.

"The door is bolted, Sir."

"It doesn't matter. Ernst, guard the rear door."

The second trooper rounded the log building and disappeared.

There was bite in the old man's voice: "Now, then, Captain, let's get things straight. Who do ye propose to remove to the reservation?"

"My orders say all Indians, Mr. Lamb."

"My wife is Siksika."

"I suggest that you accompany her there and make her comfortable there, Sir."

"My daughters are half white."

"You would not want to tear them away from their men."

Peter exclaimed, "Those aren't marriages, Joe. He's a squaw man. They all take squaws and discard them."

The journalist found himself peering into the black bore of the Henry, and paled.

The captain glared at his brother.

"Mr. Newsman Partridge," said the old man, "Aspen has been my woman for thirty-two years and none other. For her I paid the traditional bride price. Five ponies, one rifle, and more. She was given away in marriage according to the custom of her people by a fine old man who resides, even now at the age of about eighty, in the lodge yonder."

Something had changed in the old man's crevassed face. That blue eye, mild as it had been, burned icy and unblinking even as those gaunt old hands clenched the Henry in anticipation of its recoil, though it remained tucked under his arm.

"We apologize, Mr. Lamb," said the captain.

The journalist remained silent.

The one-eyed glare did not dissolve.

"Captain, every person at this post is kin to me, either by blood or by marriage. I will assume responsibility for them all, eh?"

"My orders, Sir—"

"Orders, yes. Orders. To the letter. There are,

here, five, six able-bodied Blackfeet males with which to terrorize the armies of the Republic. The rest are very old, such as Grandfather Singing Bird and Grandmother Prairie Dog Song. Others are women, children, youths . . . people who tend my flocks and gardens, who herd my sheep and watch over my horses. A menace indeed to General Terry."

"I agree, Sir, they pose no—"

"The old ones will likely succumb, if that matters to ye."

"I sympathize, Mr. Lamb, but my orders—"

"Ye'r orders. Ye'r orders. Have ye a brain and a will? Are ye a man, Sir, fit to lead? A Carthaginian peace."

"Sir?"

"Total destruction, Captain. Advocated by Cato the Elder and achieved in the Third Punic War."

Peter stared at the old man, hang-jawed.

"I'm sorry, Sir, but I have no choice."

"No choice have ye. A small spirit in a sorry career. Ye will go far in the army. Ye show all the attributes. Ye have a brigadier general mind. A choice, yes. A choice. Take my trade rifles if ye must to appease your rapacious superiors, but leave my people alone. Take the young men if you must, but leave the old and the women and the children to tend the herds and gardens. Choice, Sir, is the possession of thinking men."

Captain Partridge sighed. Then: "Private Pinski.

Take your rifles to that rise on the left flank. Private Grouard, take your rifles to the cottonwoods on the right flank. Place the lodges in your field of fire."

Three soldiers peeled off to the left, and three others to the right. The ones on the right would remain on a level with the creek and the lodges, but those on the left would be on high ground directly overlooking the Blackfeet village.

"That is my answer, Lamb. From now on, you will follow my orders exactly. First, you will surrender that Henry to Private Fiske there. Secondly, you will inform those Indians that we will move in one hour."

The old man's face blackened. "That's not time enough to dismantle lodges, load travois, harness horses, and—"

"Indians can abandon a camp in minutes, Lamb."

"And leave everything behind, yes. Ye are sending them to the reservation naked."

Lamb stared cold-eyed at the skinny trooper with the sharp Adam's apple who approached to collect the Henry rifle.

The rifle arced savagely and its stock smashed into the youth's ear, knocking him senseless. Peter jammed his hand down upon his Colt's and fired a shot that grazed the old man's cheek, bringing blood up among the white hairs of his beard. The Henry swung again, this time smashing the jaw of the newsman's gelding. The horse squealed and reared and sprayed blood from its shattered jaw and loosened teeth. Partridge landed in a heap, and rolled free from the plunging horse.

With that, the old man stalked off, deliberately exposing his back to the troopers as an act of contempt. His heart raced and his old arms trembled. There was red blood, equine and human, on the stock of his Henry. He heard shouting behind him and the crack of a pistol and more shouting that sounded like the captain roundly scolding his brother. And then he was around the house, stalking past the staring guard at the rear door, on down to the laughing creek and on, on rubbery old legs, to his daughters and their husbands and his grandchildren without number and Grandfather Singing Bird and Grandmother Prairie Dog Song; on to his kin, whose liquid brown eyes stared at his bloody beard with fear. His cheek smarted. It was his left cheek, the one beneath the eye patch. He still had half a face, he mused.

Aspen was safe in the bolted house for the moment. These people here among the lodges were not safe. He noted with some satisfaction that his horse herd was here, that his white medicine horse was saddled and ready. He spotted his daughter Faith, but Hope was gone. Some of the young men were gone, including his sons-in-law Turtle and Standing Bear. And several youths too. That was good.

"Blood of my blood," he rasped. "The soldiers

have come to take ye to the reservation. The star chiefs, Terry and Gibbon, have commanded it. I have told the captain chief who came here that the Blackfeet are not at war. But the captain says he must do this, and take away our hunting rifles as well, and the weapons in my trading post, so that we can not make meat."

Averted eyes and caught breath, the Blackfeet way of expressing horror, greeted his words.

"They want us to leave immediately," he added. "Even before Father Sun climbs to the top of the sky."

"We cannot do this," said Black Wolf, his stout, gray brother-in-law. "We will starve there on maggot meat, like the others."

It was a grim prediction. Then: "Will they shoot us like the Eagle Chief Baker did to the Piegan?"

"It is possible," replied Lamb. He stared up the west slope where the black barrels glinted.

"We could run," said Black Wolf. "Our horses are ready and the young men would keep the bluebellies busy."

"And never return," said Lamb. "And lose all ye have here. And be fugitives, at war."

"It would not be the first time," retorted Black Wolf.

The silence curdled Lamb's soul.

"They would like ye to run. They are waiting for ye to run so they can shoot ye down like ducks. Many of ye would die."

"Perhaps death is best," Black Wolf replied. "Death now rather than slow death on the reservation."

The old man shook his head. "It would be best to go there for now. Come back later when the trouble is over. But I will ask the captain chief for time for ye to take down ye'r lodges. I will tell him that we will leave in the morning, not now. Then we will return and rebuild here. That is the only way. Other ways mean death. Is that acceptable?"

"You have spoken," said Black Wolf. "You know the heart of the bluebelly chief. But once our rifles are taken, will they slaughter us?"

A wave of weakness swept through the old man. "I don't think so," he muttered. "Not with young men in the hills, and Aspen—who is a good shot—at a loophole in the post."

There was nothing more to say. Resistance would be death for these people, for Aspen, for his girls, and for himself.

He trudged back along the glistening creek, in the shadow of the cottonwoods, with a weariness upon him. He would talk with Aspen next.

"Private!" he called at the door.

"Suh?"

"Private, this Henry is my own. It goes into that post and it comes out. Understand?"

"My orders, Suh, are to prevent any firearm from—"

"Orders will make ye very dead."

He knocked and Aspen opened and then bolted the massive door behind him. With the heavy shutters closed the rooms were steeped in gloom.

She smiled the smile that always nourished him, and he hugged her.

"They are taking us to the reservation."

"I know. I heard." She had begun to probe his cheek with her fingers and stanch the blood.

"And taking our trade guns."

"There are only three," she said.

He was pleased. She had done it without being asked. Beneath their bed was a stone-lined cache under a well-concealed trapdoor.

She padded into the disordered bedroom ahead of him and he peered into the dank hollow. A dozen or so trade rifles stood there; powder and balls, and barrels of other things, perhaps a quarter of their stock in trade.

"Well done, old woman," he said softly. They lowered the wood slabs and swept dust back into the cracks and slid the heavy home-carpentered bed with its buffalo robes over the cache.

"Now we go die," she said. "I am glad to have good life with you, Lamb of God."

He glared at her, then melted. Briefly he explained that he intended to delay the trip until dawn so the lodges could be loaded in an orderly way.

She laughed. "Time come now. We go to the Sandhills now. The bluebellies will find an excuse to shoot us."

He replied gravely, his legs trembling. "I will talk to the captain now. The People will leave in the morning but not now. If anything should happen—I have lived a good life and a long one. Ye made it good and ye made it long. Bury me on a scaffold in the manner of ye'r people. Then do what ye can. This place will be ye'rs, and Faith's and Hope's if ye can keep it." He smiled. "I came here because it was beautiful. I took ye for wife because ye be beautiful."

He pressed a gnarled hard hand over her soft bronze ones and then slid to the rear door and opened it swiftly.

The private eyed him nervously but let him pass. He padded to the front of the post and into the sunny meadow beyond. The soldier he had clubbed was sitting up. The newsman with the knicker britches stood. The captain remained mounted.

The old man slid the bore of the Henry around until it pointed at the captain.

"It is arranged. The Siksika will leave in the morning," he rasped. "They will spend the afternoon dismantling lodges and packing. They will not resist. I will go with them, with my wife. Ye may enter the post now and collect the few trade rifles. I will spend the afternoon packing my trade goods so my home can be abandoned without loss."

"Sorry, Lamb, they're leaving in an hour. And

you're under arrest for striking a soldier and destroying an army mount. You're going to Fort Shaw manacled."

Richard Lamb whirled, but too late. Strong arms pinioned him from behind. He felt his Henry slide to earth, and a moment later he was there too, and chained cuffs clamped over his old wrists.

"Thought you could defy the U.S. Army, did you, old wildman?" jeered Peter Partridge. "Your name is going to be featured in the *New York Herald*."

"I never thought of anything but the safety and comfort of those I love," the old man said softly, so softly they had to strain to hear him. "But will ye write that up?"

Peter had his story. From his duffel he withdrew a field desk and foolscap and pencil and began his dispatch. He would wire it later from Fort Benton.

June 17, UPPER MUSSELSHELL, Montana Territory: A platoon of mounted rifles from Fort Shaw today captured a large band of savages of the Blackfeet tribe, under the leadership of a white renegade and pirate, one Richard Lamb.

The platoon, under the leadership of Captain Joseph Partridge of Albany, encountered fierce resistance from the eighty or so savages who declined to abandon their barbarous life to enjoy the protection and safety of the U.S. Government and its reservation agents.

Lamb, an elderly, ferocious one-eyed brigand and escapee, trafficked in arms to the savages and fostered other vices among them. It is believed by the army's far west command that Lamb's rifles, which he traded for peltries, had armed hostile Sioux and Cheyenne, including those that massacred Colonel Custer.

In spite of great forbearance on the part of Captain Partridge and his men, Lamb resisted and was finally subdued and manacled after a plot to massacre the platoon was revealed and foiled by the alert captain. Lamb will be tried by a military tribunal at Fort Shaw, rather than turned over to civil authorities.

He and his vermin-ridden cohorts are being escorted to the reservation in the northern part of the Territory. There were no casualties, thanks to the alert leadership of Captain Partridge.

# CHAPTER 4

Aspen knew that her time had come; it was her medicine saying it. She was not a medicine woman, but this was something she knew. The old man had respected her medicine, and once, long ago, it had saved their lives when she had awakened in the night and told her man that a horse-stealing party of Sioux would be at the creek at dawn. He had grumbled, but they had folded their small lodge and headed straight uphill rather than linger near the stream. From a bluff a mile away they had watched her medicine come true.

Now she knew the darkness would come soon. She would go to the Sandhills. She did not know how this would happen or whether others would die too. Perhaps they all would. The blue-coat soldiers had murder-eyes, some of them. It was one thing to make war on the despicable Crow and Shoshone and Sioux, and to steal horses and take captives and have a good satisfying torture of prisoners, and burn them with brands snatched from the fire. These things were the way of the Siksika. But the white soldiers that crawled the earth like columns of ants were mysteries, and she could not fathom their purposes. They were sinister, and had secret intentions that no child of the red races could comprehend.

Her man was a mystery too, but more like the Siksika than these bluecoats. She was glad that she had caught his eye years ago and that her father had consented. It was a proud thing to be a trapper's woman, even if this trapper was graying when his blue eye turned to her.

Cautiously she peered from a slit window that served as a loophole. She had seen and heard all that transpired. Now her man was sitting in the grass, his wrists in black iron bracelets linked by chain. It was a strange thing to do to an old man, she thought; as if they were afraid of him. She saw his medicine strong upon him and knew that he was unbroken as he sat in the sun.

Most of the soldiers were gone: three were on the bluff to the west, three more stood amid some trees to the east. There were guards outside her doors. The others, and the soldier chief, and the strange one in short pants, were there beside her man.

She did not know what to do, but Father Sun would show her. She was a good shot with her own repeater carbine and could kill two or three bluecoats and barricade herself in the post, as her man had showed her. But that made no sense. The bluecoats would kill her man and her people in the lodges and then break in and kill her. No, she would die, but perhaps she could arrange her dying so that her man would be freed. Then her people could escape to the far north, to the land of the Great Mother across the waters and of the Cree cousins who were sometimes a part of the Blackfeet alliance. But that was a cold, bog-ridden country, where the living was hard.

She closed her eyes a moment to ask the help of her spirit counsellor, the wily magpie, and she saw the black and white bird land deftly on the captain chief's nose and peck at his eyes. Then she knew. She would not be polite and offer the bluebellies the hospitality of her home, as was the Siksika custom. She would taunt the bluecoat soldiers, and the bluecoat chief especially, to their destruction. Had she not just heard her man insult the bluecoat captain? She did not know these bluecoats very well, but some instinct told her she could incite them, that they did not have the clean spiritual power of her own people. She sensed that they defied their own God rather than thanking Him or honoring Him the way the Siksika honored Father Sun in a great and solemn ceremony and dance each year.

She would taunt them just the way Siksika women taunted the prisoners brought to camp. She had no means to harm their flesh, so she would cut away the bits and pieces of their spirit—what her man called soul—until she made them no-longer-men. Even her man in the black chains seemed to do that to the captain chief who eyed him so nervously. Before she was done, they would wish they had never come here. Life was more than bullets; it was will.

She met them at the door, unbolting it even before they knocked, and she stared into the gray eyes of this captain chief, and then at the brother in short pants. She saw what she expected to see. Her man had been right about them.

"You have come for the guns," she said. "Come take the guns so they will not be pointed against you."

"Madam," began Joseph Partridge, "good day. I am glad you have not chosen to resist. It would go worse for your husband and your people."

"Indeed it would go worse," she agreed. "I am glad that is settled. You have him helpless there in great chains because you truly know that the old man is as dangerous to you as a thousand armies."

Captain Partridge smiled benignly. "Dangerous? No. Simply a precaution taken with all military prisoners. This, madam, is my brother Peter Partridge, a newspaper reporter in a great city in the East."

"New York, yes, I heard you tell my man. From the window."

"We are under orders, madam, to confiscate such arms as you have here."

"Come in and take them," she said. "Then you will feel much safer."

The short-pants man, the one who wrote the talking words, was staring at her, and she was conscious of her great beauty. Even at forty-nine winters she was unusually beautiful, she knew—tall, slim, with brown eyes that laughed above the sharp planes of her brown cheeks. Her full mouth still contained all her white, even, shining teeth. She knew she was beautiful now because she had lived wisely and happily and because she laughed a great deal. When she was young it was because her mother and father created her that way, but now it was because she had lived joyfully.

"Mr. Peter Partridge," she said, "you have shot at my man and torn the flesh of his cheek and spilled his blood. You have shot at an old man and now you are making big boasts inside yourself and entering my house as if it is your house. This thing that you did, it is a great deed to tell in New York, yes?"

"Madam—"

"Yes, a great deed. What the Siksika call counting coup. You will tell the women of New York how you shot a trader—perhaps you will call him a savage man—and they will admire you. You will write a story too and be honored in your city."

"Enough!" snapped Captain Partridge. "Be silent, madam. Now, the trade guns—why are there only three? And caplocks at that?"

"What do you suppose?" she retorted. "Do you suppose the Siksika and the devil Crow are rich and can buy new guns that shoot streams of bullets? These are for hunting, not war."

Partridge glared at the shelves and at the passage to the private quarters at the rear. "Search!" he snapped at a private beside him, who scurried into the kitchen.

"You will take all powder and ball even for hunting? And the guns in the lodges too?"

"Those are my orders."

"You want Siksika to starve."

"You'll be fed by the Indian Agent."

She laughed wickedly. "Maybe you shoot Siksika now and save the trouble, eh? Die fast rather than slow."

"We have no intentions—"

"That carbine there. I own it. Shoots good."

"I'm sorry, madam, but it goes too."

"It shoots good. You shoot lots of Siksika children. Lots of Siksika grandchildren. Nephews and nieces in the lodges. What you say, eh? You kill everyone off, save lots of trouble. Start big battle and your brother have good story to put in newspaper. Make you a big hero if you tell it just right. Kill old white man who helps Siksika, yes? Big hero then."

The captain glared at her. "We have no intention of—"

"Yes you do. In your eyes I see it, killer-man. The death eye. You shoot maybe me first. I die now."

"What I'll do is lock you in a room here if you don't stop babbling such nonsense."

"You do that, killer-man. Then go kill friendly Indians, old men and old women."

The private emerged from the rear. "Nothing," he said. "I searched it good."

"Newspaper man," she leered, "no good story, eh? No guns captured. No big pile of powder and ball. Only one old man, a few Blackfeet Indians, and papoose. Papoose is white-man word, not

Blackfeet. No good story. We be like cattle you take to market. You want good story? Start a war. You got a big sixgun to shoot old men. Start a war. Then you feel big, eh? Big medicine in newspaper. You shoot me first, eh? I die, and then the big story starts."

There was something in the startled newsman's eyes that told her she had counted coup, plumbed something dark in him, some truth. She could tell that the man in short pants was wishing for a war.

"Watch her," Captain Partridge ordered. "I'm going back there for a look. I can't believe there are only three muzzle-loading caplocks and a carbine in the place."

He disappeared.

She eyed Peter contemplatively.

He stared out the slit window at the old man sitting quietly in the grass.

"Why are you afraid of the old man?"

"Why? I'm not a bit—"

"You afraid. You shoot him, and put him in chains."

"That's nonsense."

"You afraid because he has more truth in him than you. And more white-man words from books. He's all truth and you no truth at all."

Peter's face flamed red with rage.

"You afraid maybe the old man go talk to chiefs, maybe got friends in Washington City that listen. He so full of truth they always listen, and maybe he says bad things about the soldiers and the captain and you, maybe tell the whole world that you are a no good sonofabitch."

The private grinned.

"Maybe you kill old man first, eh? Then he can't talk to big chiefs with white-man words. Then shoot the Injuns. Nobody believes lousy redskin Injuns, all liars and drunks, no good. Then you make big story, brave soldiers kill enemies by hundreds, thousands."

Peter grinned. "Preposterous but amusing. I'll do a story about you, madam. Keep on talking."

"I'll give you a story, newsman. Big horseapple story like the Crow tell."

"Did you learn such language from your ruffian husband, madam?"

"Hell no, it's old Siksika word. We got it from mountain men. I got lots more, too."

The captain returned, irked.

"They're hidden somewhere. Maybe in the lodges. We'll search the grounds. You—" he pointed to Aspen, "come translate."

"You get old man to translate. English like sour cherries in my mouth."

The captain nodded to the private. "Go get Lamb. They're both going. Take these old caplocks and the powder out to the pack horses when you go."

The youth rattled out.

Aspen pushed her luck. "Pretty soon you be

big army hero, get stars or eagles on shoulders, eh? My man says you got the head for it."

"One more word, woman, and I'll take measures."

"Take anything. It's a good day to die."

He stared at her, puzzled.

Richard Lamb entered, followed by a trooper. His eye carefully scanned the shelves.

"Well, Captain?"

"We'll search the lodges now. You and your squaw will come along and translate."

"Very well, then."

The small party walked up the creek: three soldiers, the captain, the newsman, and the Lambs. The old man trudged awkwardly, his manacled hands in front of him.

"This place," he said to no one in particular, "was a favorite summering place of the Piegans, the Pekunny they call themselves . . . too far south for the Blackfeet proper or the Blood. They came here every summer until they were decimated by smallpox . . . and later Baker's disease. It's a sacred place, a medicine place to them. Religious traditions here. I don't suppose the First Amendment has any application here, eh, Captain?"

The captain stared ahead.

"I thought not. Out beyond the frontier anyone can do anything. The Ten Commandments are null and void west of the hundredth meridian, eh?"

The newsman eyed him speculatively.

Aspen's bronze kin were waiting somberly. Grandfather Singing Bird and Grandmother Prairie Dog Song, and her numberless grandchildren and nephews and nieces and kin. Nothing had been moved. No lodge dismantled. Before them stood Black Wolf, Aspen's brother, his iron hair laced with gray. Their eyes were upon only one thing, the manacles that bound Richard Lamb's wrists in front of him, an obscene viola-tion of the old man.

The captain stared back. There was no weapon visible among these people, but his hand hovered near his revolver and so did the hands of his enlisted men.

"Tell them that we will now search the lodges for weapons and that we shall escort them immediately to the Blackfeet reservation. They are to have their horses and wagons ready by the time we finish searching the lodges."

The old man told them quietly.

"No," said Black Wolf in English.

"Who is this man, Lamb?"

"I am Black Wolf, brother-in-law of Mister Lamb," the Indian replied, also in English.

"Tell your people to mount their horses, Black Wolf. You have no choice in the matter."

"We have chosen to die. A fast death is better than a slow one."

The captain was perplexed. "What's he talking about, Lamb?"

"He's talking about death next winter. Ye be sending these people north with naught but the skins on their backs, with no weapons to make meat, and into the hands of an Indian agent so corrupt that his reports don't even mention the number of Blackfeet that die each day of starvation or the pox."

"I have my orders. We will move them bodily if they won't move themselves."

Aspen jeered. "You get to be eagle chief quick quick."

He glared at her.

The search detail disappeared into the first lodge, Black Wolf's, and emerged empty-handed. Each of the seven lodges was searched, but no weapons, save for a bow and a quiver of arrows, were found. Captain Partridge stormed back.

"Lamb, you said there were five or six young men. Where are they?"

"They are gone," said Richard Lamb.

The captain glared. "Where?"

"Gone," said Lamb.

The captain cuffed him and the old man, unbalanced by the manacles, fell.

"That was good. That make you star chief. Hit old man, yes," Aspen hissed.

The captain whirled and cuffed her as well. She staggered and then crawled to Richard Lamb.

"Time come now," she said. "I'm ready to go to Sandhills. You follow orders."

The old man stared at her.

"Lamb, you tell your squaw to be silent or I'll remove her," snapped Partridge.

The old man struggled to his feet. "She is my wife," he replied quietly, "and she may say what she will."

A certain look passed between the manacled bloody man and the woman on the grass. She felt tears coming but refused to let them well up. She would not wail now while her man still lived.

"I think, Sir," said Lamb, "that ye be at an impasse. These people will not move unless ye permit them to dismantle their households and prepare for the long journey."

It was Peter Partridge who answered. "Nonsense, Joe, a little taste of the bayonet will start them moving fast enough."

"We will not go," said Black Wolf.

"He's bluffing," said Peter.

Black Wolf sat down and so did the others, a small solemn group of bronze children and women and old men.

The captain addressed his brother curtly. "We'll shed no blood if we can help it." He turned to the man behind him. "Private! Find harness for those two wagons. We'll haul these people on wagons."

"Those are my wagons," said Lamb. "And ye'll not have them to use."

"Sorry, Lamb, I'm requisitioning them."

"They won't carry half of the people here."

"The rest will ride or walk."

"Or die," said Lamb.

"I won't shed blood."

"You already have. Before the day over you change your mind. You getting mad, got killer-eyes now," jeered Aspen.

"Woman, I told you, be quiet," the captain barked.

"You so mad pretty soon you kill friendly Indians. Great story, newspaperman write it up good. Kill squaws and old men. Big famous bluebelly."

The captain had enough. "Corporal Rudeen! Escort this squaw to the post and keep her under guard. Hand me your rifle first, and your bayonet."

The corporal handed Partridge the two weapons, and the captain snapped the bayonet into position.

Aspen felt the bluecoat's arms drag her up and haul her bodily back to the trading post. She did not struggle. Instead, she turned her head back to watch, as the captain pressed the naked bayonet into the ribs of her brother Black Wolf who sat impassively in the sun, even as his sky blue calico shirt turned black with blood.

# CHAPTER 5

"Ye'll kill him before he'll move," rasped Richard Lamb. He was dizzy and had a raging thirst from the fierce sun.

Sweat dripped from the brow of Captain Joseph Partridge. A steady gout of blood oozed from the bayonet wound in Black Wolf's ribs. The blade had been shoved an inch or more. Black Wolf's face had turned to granite, and only the dark eyes, flashing cold fire, betrayed any sensation at all.

"Ye've pierced a lung, ye have," the old man added. The wound was frothing. There was a gray pallor beneath the golden surface of Black Wolf's flesh.

The old man stared toward the post, where Corporal Rudeen was dragging Aspen. She was neither resisting nor speaking. He knew it was unlike her to speak. Her insults to the soldiers were calculated, and it was plain to him that the barbs had struck home or they would have borne her jabs unheedingly. It amazed him. Aspen was the soul of hospitality and Blackfeet decorum to any guest in their home or any customer in the trading room. Rudeen pushed her into the trading post, and it was good. She would be safe there.

The other soldier was hunting for harness. He would find it soon enough in the log shed. The wagons, which the old man used to haul trade goods, hides, and pelts, might hold the children. But they could hold no others.

He stared at his old, veined hands in their black iron caskets, hands weak from the years, and he wished he might once more be young. But he was not. His legs quaked. But he had one thing still— an educated mind. A mind schooled in the best New England college and schooled again in the Rocky Mountain college, where every fur trapper graduated . . . or died. He had the tools of words and thoughts, the cutting edge of perception and will. Whatever he achieved now, if anything, would be solely the fruit of a disciplined mind and a life on the frontier and in the wilderness. Actually, Aspen had given him this clue—she had perceived vanity and ambition in these Partridges and had started to slice it away until . . . what? Until they made a mistake.

So then, he thought; their character might be a key.

"Ye'll not earn the favor of your superiors, boy, if ye show up at the agency with a wagonload of corpses."

The captain whirled. "You stay out of it, Lamb."

"Ye have orders to deliver live Indians, boy. Or don't ye follow orders, eh?"

Stung, the captain jerked the bayonet free and stared at Black Wolf. A faint, pained glint rose in the eyes of the gray man.

"Bind that wound," the captain barked. "We'll truss up all of you and haul you like cordwood if you won't walk."

Black Wolf sat impassively, the lifeblood still gouting from his ribs.

"Peter, dammit, bind up that Indian."

"That's not my job. That's an army job. I'm here for stories."

Joseph glared at his brother and summoned the remaining private, Ernst.

"Find a long rag and bind him. There's bolts of tradecloth in the post."

"A dollar a yard, boy," said Lamb. "Two a yard for the army."

"We're requisitioning it."

"It seems that all my property has suddenly become the army's. Would ye call that theft, boy?"

"I'd call it getting the job done."

"Surely there are easier ways of doing it than sticking bayonets into people."

"Not another word out of you, Lamb!"

The old man sat quietly a moment. His body quaked and his dizziness made him reel, even sitting down. Contemplatively he eyed the newsman, the dandy in knickerbockers.

"Mr. Newsman," he began. "How are ye going to write all this up? Are ye going to tell them that today ye'r captain brother stuck a bayonet into the ribs of a sitting Indian?"

"What difference does it make to you? I doubt that you could read any of it anyway. Where'd you get your learning—around trapper campfires?"

"Ye've not answered my question, boy."

"Why bother? I have no reason to answer the questions of a renegade Indian-loving trader . . . and traitor."

"I've asked ye if ye plan to write the truth, all the truth, boy, and ye give me no answer."

"I write the truth as I see it," Peter retorted coldly.

"I see," said the old man. "It works fine if there's no one around to contradict ye. The word of Indians, dead or alive, won't cramp ye'r style much. Neither will the word of an old renegade white trader, eh, boy?"

"I will write what I see."

"Such as this torture."

"He's obviously a hostile, disobeying army orders."

"Yes, ye have now made him such, I grant. Will ye write it that way or will ye turn a skunk into a rose?"

"I will write according to ethical standards that are too complicated for simple people outside of my profession to understand."

"Lies, boy, lies. Ye be a paid liar, eh?"

"Lamb, shut your mouth! That's an order!" shouted the captain.

The old man fixed the officer with his fierce blue eye. "Will ye also lie, boy? Lie to your commanding officers, eh?"

"I'll report things exactly as they happened, and devote much of it to you."

"Mighty nice of ye, boy. If ye'll report things exactly as they are, I'll affirm it to your superiors, eh?"

"You'll do nothing of the kind."

The old man lapsed into silence again. Black Wolf's wound had been bound, the bleeding had ceased, and the stocky Indian lay in the grass. Near the log shed, the private was assembling the harness. He had caught a couple of horses and had tied them to a rail there. The horses were not broke to harness.

Peter Partridge was looking worried. "Lamb," he said, "can you read and write?"

"Enough to make out a lie in print, Mr. Newsman."

Partridge reddened. "I don't think you're being very square with me, Lamb. You be square with me and I'll let you off easy in my stories, in spite of your crimes."

"My reputation among New York readers is of no concern to me, boy."

"It's not New York readers I'm thinking about, Lamb. It's the army tribunal that's going to examine your case at Fort Shaw. My testimony could get you off light."

"I see," said Richard Lamb. "Bear in mind, boy, that I am old and see God on the horizon."

The newsman was taken aback. "What's that supposed to mean?" he asked.

"It means, boy, 'Render unto Caesar the things that are Caesar's and unto God the things that are God's.' Truth is God's."

The newsman was palpably alarmed. "You are a dangerous man, Lamb, and I will make sure it is understood that you are demented."

Richard Lamb grinned. "Dangerous, boy? I am a manacled old man. What danger do I pose to ye? Other than as a witness, eh?"

Peter didn't answer. Instead, he loped off to join the captain, who was hunting for any pony that looked like a draft horse.

The old man's concerned eye fell upon Black Wolf, the widower, the brother-in-law, lying all alone in pain. Flies were crawling over the blood-soaked bandaging.

"Ye were brave before Father Sun," Lamb whispered in Piegan.

"I can hardly breathe," the man rasped. "The steel went deep but I would not let the bluecoats see."

"Ye need help and I must get ye into the post where Aspen can help ye. Can ye walk?"

"Yes."

"Let us go, then. They are busy with harness."

The old man stood up shakily and helped the

Indian to his feet. "Lean on me," he said. "With these bound hands I can't hold ye."

Together they stumbled along the creek, under the cottonwood leaves, past the soldiers attempting to harness a horse unbroken to harness. The private guarding Aspen eyed them apprehensively.

"What is your purpose?" breathed Black Wolf as they hobbled along.

"Purpose? Why, to stay here and live with you people. And my plan is to shame these scoundrels. They are ambitious, and that is their weakness. They want no dishonor upon their names."

"They are without vision," Black Wolf muttered.

"Lamb!" roared the captain from the wagons. "Who gave you permission—"

The old man stared. "I don't live by ye'r permission, boy. And I'm taking this man to my wife who will tend to his wound."

"You seem to forget you're under arrest."

"I've not for a moment forgotten it."

The captain glared. "Very well, then. But you stay outside where I can see you."

They hobbled past Aspen's guard at the door, who had heard the exchange. Aspen was at the door and helped her brother in.

"Wait," she said to Lamb, and a moment later thrust a mug of broth into his hands. It was what he needed. He sipped it with relish as if it were his own last supper.

"Thank ye, Aspen. We may yet succeed."

She shook her head. "They got kill look. More bayonet soon." She closed and bolted the door.

It was time for more mischief, he thought. And maybe some negotiation. He padded quietly to the wagons and watched. One dun mustang was in harness, threatening to explode. The private was backing a big sorrel into the traces of the other wagon.

"My rental fee is two dollars a wagon a day," he said.

The captain stared at the old man.

"Neither of those horses is broke to harness. If ye wreck the wagons or hurt my beasts, ye'll be responsible for the loss, eh?"

The captain continued grimly to wrestle the wild-eyed rearing horse.

"My fee for hauling Indians is a dollar a head, plus expenses. But of course they won't go unless I ask them to."

"We'll see about that," the captain gritted. "I'm loading the children. The rest will come along unless they wish to abandon the children. Or else we'll bayonet them along."

Lamb sighed. "Ye have the determination and the brains of a cannonball," he muttered, and walked slowly back to his people. The manacles pulled at his wrists and made his arms ache.

Wearily he sat down among his subdued kin, noting their solemn stares. His daughter Faith was among them, a lighter gold and blue-eyed, but otherwise with the features and build of her mother's people. It was not yet midday, he noted. He smiled at Faith, his bold blue eye resting kindly upon her. Standing Bear, her husband, was among the young men who had fled and who even now were watching events here from somewhere in the hills. Lamb hoped they would not act rashly or kill the bluecoats.

He told his people what they might expect. Mothers gazed keenly upon the children, some of them his grandchildren. To the children he said, "Do what ye will and take heart. The soldiers will not harm ye."

The young people whispered among themselves. "Be *Siksika*," he said to them, preferring the more meaningful word for Blackfeet, rather than the word *Piegan*. To be a Siksika was to be bold, fierce, proud, and indomitable.

The soldiers had a wagon readied near the post, and potbellied Corporal Rudeen was perched on the seat, reins in hand, ready for the tantrums of horses and children. But the dun horse proved docile, and he drove the rig upstream to the lodges and the huddled humanity there that would soon be ripped from its roots.

A surly Captain Partridge appeared.

"Tell the children to get in, Lamb," he barked.

"I don't give orders, boy. They are a free people and not mine to command, eh? Ask their parents, eh?"

"Then I will," the captain snarled. "Get in the wagon. Get in. You understand?" He pointed ferociously. "Get—in—wagon."

Nothing happened.

"Private Murphy, pick up that girl there and carry her."

The private slid his rifle over his shoulder and lifted the doeskin-clad girl of ten or so. Pawing Horse did not resist, but neither did she help him. He dumped her roughly in the bed and began fetching others. It was a solemn time. The wagon was a small one and soon nine children were jammed into it. Then, as if on signal, all nine bolted out like a covey of quail, running every which way, and vanishing among the lodges.

"Very funny, Lamb. You've had your joke. From now on these people obey or get hurt. Corporal, am I correct in assuming that we've a bugler in the squad?"

"Sir, Private Pinski is with the rifles above."

"Then proceed to semaphore. Are there flags?"

"No, sir."

"Never mind, I'll do it."

He faced the west first, one arm high. Then he pumped it up and down. Three small dots of men arose and trudged down the slope to Elk Creek. From the cottonwoods to the east came three more, trudging across an emerald meadow laced with fragrant blue sage. Even before they had collected at the lodges, Captain Partridge was shouting staccato orders.

"Fiske, Johnson, guard the horses and keep an eye on the hills. Some bucks are out there. Pinski—take two men and find the children. Murphy, go to the post and find some rope or cord." He glared at Lamb. "You have cord, I presume?"

Lamb sighed. "A barrel of half-inch hemp. Five cents a foot, eh?"

The old man knew he'd never be paid but he knew he was making a point, a point about the cavalier treatment of private property. And he hoped that somewhere in the captain's soul there would be a prick of conscience.

Lamb studied the self-confident captain. The man had the quality of assurance and command. He strode confidently, chest forward, faintly self-congratulatory. The old man knew that few of his barbs had even pricked the captain. The newsman in knickers, though, might prove more vulnerable. He was softer, flabbier, an obvious voluptuary, and busily writing dispatches that were probably affronts to truth. He would feel a tinge of guilt about that, but only a tinge. The man seemed to walk knickers-first as if the most important part of him were his loins.

Luke Old Coyote had quietly, almost invisibly, drifted the post's horses out beyond the lodges to the south, so subtly that it seemed almost the random drift of grazing animals. But it wasn't.

Lamb watched the last of the ponies vanish around the bend of a broad coulee, and he knew that Luke would run them fast once they were out of sight. He had started the moment the soldiers had walked down from the slope above.

The bluecoats were hunting the children now, in and out of lodges, and as fast as a soldier entered a lodge a child squirted out from its skirts at the rear. They captured a brown button of a girl at last and carried her unprotesting to the wagon and trussed her up with great coils of rope. It was a pathetic sight and it disgusted the old man. The huddled Piegans watched impassively. When the fifth child was trussed, the soldiers ran out of rope.

"There be not enough rope on earth and in heaven for your purposes," said the old man.

"Murphy! Go search the post!" The private trotted off once again.

Partridge whirled toward Lamb. "You'll by god have more rope or we'll cut these lodges into strips and bind them with hide."

"Ye need no rope a-tall," the old man replied softly. "They would all sit quietly in the wagon if I were to ask them, eh?"

"Well ask them!"

"No," said Lamb. He walked away, his legs quaking again.

"Lamb! I'm ordering you to ask them!"

The old man turned, his eye glittering, and he stared.

"I have ways of making you ask them. A little more bayonet. Or the execution of that man. Or a few lashes on your back. Just because you're old, don't suppose you're exempt from prisoner discipline."

The old man stood calmly, silently.

"I'll give you five seconds to ask them."

Lamb sighed. "If they see me acting under duress, boy, they'll not heed me, eh? If I were to ask them, it'd have to be freely, upon my judgment, eh?"

The captain glared into the old man's eye. "I'm adding your lack of cooperation to the charges, Lamb. I might have let you off easy."

The captain looked ready to explode. Lamb smelled the odor of sweat rising from the captain's wet blue armpits, and thought that this meadow usually was redolent of sweet sage, what his kin called *kak-sim-i*. He thought that when he died he would like a sprig of sweet clean sage in his hands for his burial. Or maybe he would prefer the scaffold burial of his wife's people, a gift to the sun rather than to the dark earth.

"Corporal Rudeen," the captain bawled. "Fix your bayonet. Hand your rifle to me."

The captain grabbed the weapon and faced the old man with wrath. The old man braced himself, and felt the white hot chill of the blade press into the flesh of his left ribcage, between the lowest and next-lowest ribs. There was a pressure, and then the parting of flesh, and a sharp sting, white pain, and the wetness of blood upon his hip-bone.

"Ask them!" commanded Captain Partridge.

The old man felt dizzy, and sweat broke his brow. The stink of the captain's body suffocated him. He turned to the vision of sage, one bush of the pale green sweet herb.

"If ye kill me," he muttered at last, "ye'll never get a one of these folk to the reservation. Nary a one. Unless ye kill them all first, which I see ye are ready to do. But if ye try that, ye'll die, boy. The lads above have rifles on ye all, and be looking for a reason to use them."

The captain jerked his eyes to the westward slopes.

He handed the weapon back to Corporal Rudeen.

Lamb felt a merciful release from the cold steel, though a widening pain remained. He bled. He had been *Siksika* himself, and now he sensed a victory, the first of this long and terrible day.

"Captain," he murmured, "all ye think of is force. Ye've been in the army too long."

Partridge stared at him blankly. "What's your price, Lamb? Everyone has a price, and you've held out for yours. I'll tell you now, these Injuns are going to their reservation dead or alive, so don't ask to stay here."

Lamb drew himself up on legs that almost buckled. His golden buckskin leggins were stained brown.

"There'll be time to dismantle the lodges, build travois, pack up households, put things in parfleches," he began. "We'll leave when we're ready, some time tomorrow. We'll drive some cattle with us. We'll set a pace that will not kill the grandparents. We'll be treated as friendly allies. These Piegan women will have as much right to bring their domestic things with them as any captain's wife has to bring her goods to an army post . . . And ye'll conduct yerselves, ye and the newsman, as gentlemen, eh?"

That last, the old man knew, would enrage the brothers Partridge, and might even undo it all. He glanced at Peter, who stood staring, pop-eyed. For a long moment no one spoke, and the stink of sweat filled the meadow air. The captain reddened, then his apoplexy gave way to acceptance.

Peter couldn't contain himself. "Don't do it, Joe. Don't you see? He's got you buffaloed. He's got the U.S. Army on the run. He's making a fool of you. You've got ten bayonets and all you've got to do is herd this bunch up and start them walking."

Lamb replied gently. "There are armed men in the hills. If ye want these soldiers of ye'rs to die, along with yerself, newsboy, just go ahead, eh? And if ye look around a bit, ye'll see nary a pony here, eh?"

Both Peter and the captain stared wildly. There

was not an Indian pony in sight except for the two harnessed to the wagons. The only choice the army had now was to start a death march.

"Very well, Lamb. But I'm going to get even, and don't you forget it. At Fort Shaw you'll be sorry, sorrier than you've ever been in your life."

# CHAPTER 6

Peter Partridge was irked. His brother had allowed these savages and a manacled old wildman to back him down. That was no way for a white man to behave. Worse, Joseph had rebuked Peter and had refused even to consider Peter's counsel.

What the newsman had proposed was perfectly logical. A show of force. The obvious thing to do was to pull that wounded one in the trading post out to the nearest cottonwood and execute him as a hostile. That would teach these savages the lesson they needed, and would halt this resistance to the U.S. Army.

But Joseph would have none of it. Peter thought that the old man was right: His brother went by the book and had so narrow and unimaginative a mind that he was doomed to a rule-heeding petty life.

In the long light of late afternoon, he strolled among the lodges, watching the savages prepare for the morrow's exodus. Cookfires smouldered lazily before the skin teepees, hazing the still air. Perhaps there was a story here if he could find it, or if not something suitable for the *Herald*, then an anecdote or two to tell the ladies at his elbow in Manhattan.

God, what a desolate place! And what a barbarous life, with not a pillow of comfort in it. How anyone could prefer skin teepees to solidly built homes was beyond him. The young men were still gone, but Joseph had assured him they would return with the horses as soon as they saw, from the hills, that the Siksika were unmolested.

The bronze people ignored him and he was glad of it. He didn't want those verminous savages too close. His hand was never far from his holstered .45. But these were old people and women and children and Peter felt safe enough. They all looked old. The hard life turned the young women old. They were loading their small crude things of hide and bone and feather and stone into hide parfleches, brightly dyed. The scruffy brown buffalo robes they apparently slept in were being rolled and tied with thong. A graying woman teetered down a distant slope dragging two long lodgepoles that would make a travois.

An ancient man—one Lamb had called Grandfather Singing Bird—with a face as craggy and seamed as a worn-out boot sat quietly before his sagging lodge. He alone seemed to notice Peter; his obsidian eyes never parted from Peter's face and Peter felt a primitive power radiating from the old devil; power that made him nervous . . . and envious.

Beside his lodge stood a tripod decorated with feathers, bead-work, and small animal skulls. And dangling as well were a dozen or so hairy things that Peter suddenly recognized as scalps. Human hair. Most of them were blue black. Two were a dusty brown, and one was blond.

Peter jerked his eyes away spastically, and the sight of the bivouac and his own kind, camped two hundred yards distant, calmed him. The old man Lamb was being held there and was sitting quietly in the soft grass.

There were yellow and gray curs running loose through the camp and Peter walked delicately around their piles. Occasionally an odor of human waste mingled rancidly with the smell of stews or the fine sizzling scent of roasting meat. On long, complex racks of poles, thin slices of some meat or other were being dried to make jerky. Elk, he supposed, judging from a half-cut carcass hanging from a small cottonwood nearby.

The women wore doe- or elkskin skirts, he noticed, but there was one who did not. A particularly tall young squaw was adorned in dotted red calico and a hip-length white blouse belted at the waist. Beneath her ankle-length full skirts were the traditional black moccasins of the tribe, the reason the early French trappers called them the *Pieds Noirs*. He stared at her, and found himself staring into brilliant blue eyes. Her hair, too, was not the blue-black of the others, but a deep chestnut, though it was severely braided like the hair of the other women.

A daughter of old Lamb, Peter thought. He must have sired her late in life. And a striking one at that—tall, thin, with those bold cheekbones and sky-kissed eyes peering wisely at him. A stunning daughter. And she'd speak English, too. Maybe he could get a story about this half-breed maiden.

He approached, all his discontents forgotten, the ladies' man in him seeking conquest and amusement. She watched him coming impassively, and just as he was about to speak she vanished into her lodge.

He waited. She did not reappear. There were half-packed bundles on the matted grass outside, but she remained cloistered.

Well then, the mountain will go to Mahomet, he thought. There was a low oval entrance hung with a skin door. This he lifted, and he entered and waited until his eyes adjusted.

It was actually less gloomy than he had supposed, with light piercing translucently through the buffalo cowhide.

Faith stood quietly at the farthest distance.

"Do you enter a white woman's house without knocking?" Her voice was husky and low; she had her father's mellifluous diction.

"Why—this isn't a home. It's a . . . a shelter," he stumbled.

"It's my home. Please leave."

He laughed. "You call this a home? Yes, I suppose you would, not having known any other."

"I've asked you to leave."

"Now, squaw woman, I have no intention of doing that, at least not for the moment. It will depend on you. If I get what I want, I will then leave."

"My husband would not—"

"Where is he?"

"He will be here soon."

"Husband, eh? How many other squaws has he?"

She was silent.

He studied her in the soft warm light. She was uncommonly pretty. Exciting even, in some barbaric way. He felt a stirring of desire.

"Your father is Lamb?"

She said nothing.

"Of course he is. Same eyes, same English. Well, if you're good to me, maybe I'll go easy on him when we get to Fort Shaw."

"What is it you want?" She gazed stonily into his face, unblinking.

His heart pounded a bit.

"Why . . . an interview for the *Herald*. About the life of the, uh—the life of squaws in your tribe."

"No. You may leave now."

"I'll leave when I choose. You're a captive of the U.S. Army, you know."

"I didn't know. Does your army always capture its allies?"

"Captain Partridge has concluded this band is hostile."

She smiled bitterly. "For wanting to stay here peacefully?"

"For resisting."

"You will leave now or I will tell your brother you are here."

She began to circle around him to the door, but he blocked her passage, grinning. Something dark blazed in her eyes. He clamped her wrist, arresting her movement.

"Sit down. I'm going to interview you for the *Herald* story."

She sat silently.

"Tell me your name. Tell me everything you know about your father."

"I doubt that the private life of an Indian trader is important."

"If you will talk about him, I might make it easy for him at Fort Shaw."

"And if I don't?"

"He'll rot in a stockade until he dies."

Something flashed across her face, a faltering, a love for her father, and he knew he had her then. But she surprised him.

"There is nothing to say. Your readers would be

bored. Now if you do not leave, I will go tell your brother the captain that you have held me prisoner here by force in my own lodge."

Peter laughed. "I will tell him you invited me in—for your own savage purposes."

"I have nothing to say."

"Come now, a little story. The life of a trader family and some Blackfeet customs. How did your father turn into such a—what shall I say?—uncivilized man?"

"Our life is not your property, newsman. It does not belong to you or your readers. I am not for sale."

"Then I will write about you anyway, without your cooperation."

"It will be lies."

"It will be my impressions."

She was silent.

"Tell me, when did your father turn against his own kind?"

"He never did. He . . ." She lapsed into silence.

"Why does he run guns to hostiles?"

She stared.

"He could be in trouble for that, you know. Unless I tell Joseph to let him off."

"I will not talk to you anymore," she said sullenly.

He badgered her for a few more minutes, but she remained mute, gravely meeting his eyes but saying not a word. He got nothing, not even the thread of a story. Finally, he rose.

"I'll make it hard for you. You'll regret this. You'll wish you had talked," he warned.

Stupid squaw, he thought as he ducked past the lodge flap and into the bright sun. He glared at the lodges and these savages and stalked toward the bivouac. He fumed. He'd get the goods on Lamb even if he had to slap it out of someone. Stupid squaw. He'd fix her wagon good.

A story was building in his mind, and the more he visualized it, the more excited he got. Somewhere, the Sioux and Cheyenne that had slaughtered the Custer command had gotten the guns to do it. Thousands of guns. Where had they come from? Most, surely, from right here! From Lamb's trading post. Hundreds, maybe thousands, of rifles, carbines, and old flintlocks and cap-locks. He'd prove it even if he had to rattle the teeth of Lamb and his women to get it.

It'd be a story, all right. A renegade trader whose reckless gun running had led to the greatest defeat in U.S. military history, and during the nation's centennial year, too. The country was still looking for reasons and causes. Official commissions and inquiries were still in process, sifting facts and allegations. Even now, Libby Custer was stirring the pot in the East, canonizing her late husband and heaping coals of fire on the whole army, on Major Reno, and on other targets of her ire. A story about this renegade Lamb would be front-page news, and would be reprinted clear across the country.

His heart pounded. He would be famous. The facts were obvious; anyone could see that. All he had to do was fill in a little bit where these savages were reluctant to talk. It would be a sensation, and his brother would get the honors for rounding up the old gun-runner. There would be a sensational trial, too, with federal prosecutors from Washington City, and that would be yet another story to cover to make a name for himself.

But he needed more information.

He swerved toward the post and barged past the guard. He would start with Lamb's squaw, and would get her to talking, by god, if he had to pound her into it.

There was no one in the trading room. Light streamed through a small window with real glass in it. The shelves behind the counter seemed curiously empty.

The squaw, Aspen, appeared at the door leading to the private quarters. He remarked again her handsomeness.

"Newspaperman!" she exclaimed. "You have come to visit, and I have brewed some tea. You want some? You want to talk, maybe? I like talk. Lonely in here."

"Tea, yes. And I'd like to look around. I'm writing a story about your, ah, man and his trading post."

He didn't await permission. It never occurred to him that he was in someone's home, or that the rules of etiquette applied here. He circled the counter and barged into the back rooms.

"Pour the tea and I'll be with you in a minute," he commanded.

He plunged into a tiny alcove that appeared to be an office. There were some shelved books and a crude desk of whipsawed plank. And on it was a deerskin-bound ledger with lined pages. He flipped it open and found exactly what he hoped to find, an accounting of every transaction, every trade, written in an even, disciplined hand and occasionally blotted. Lamb used quills rather than steel nibs, and probably made his own ink. There was a wooden box of brass tokens on the desk, no doubt used for trade.

Yes, here it all was:

June 17. One four-point blanket, for three tanned elk hides.

June 16. One Sharps, .54 calibre, used, for five tanned buffalo robes, prime. 1/2-lb. powder, 50 caps, one bar galena, for 12 beaver plews, 4, prime, 7 good, one summer pelt. . . .

He tucked the ledger under his arm. He would examine it at leisure later. It was a story of national interest, and that was all that mattered.

He glanced around, wondering what more he might uncover. Some old newspapers were yellowing in a corner. A pair of spectacles, quills, an ink bottle, and some blotters made of soft tanned skins littered the desk.

"You taking big book?" asked Aspen. "That tell the whole story. You see how it goes here, every trade, yes? Then you bring it back. It's not yours. It goes with post, and is property of Richard Lamb."

"I'm sorry, madam, but I'm going to take it for a while. It tells me important things about the trading here."

She shrugged and smiled. "Maybe that's a good idea. You look at everything, see how we trade. Good story for you and readers of the talking signs. Come have tea."

He followed her into the kitchen where two porcelain cups steamed on a plank table.

"Now you tell me what you want," she said.

"I want to write a story about Richard Lamb and this trading post, and make him famous to all the white men."

"True story?"

"Of course." He sipped.

"Not much story," she said. "Mostly we grow cattle and vegetables for the mines at Helena and Butte and Marysville and Maiden."

"Tell me about it. I think my readers would like to know."

"Maybe I will, maybe I won't. Maybe I trade you something for it."

"Trade?"

"Sure, newspaperman, trade. I give you something, you give me something." She grinned.

"What do you want?" He felt a prickle of delight. This would be easy.

"You tell your brother captain chief to take the irons off Richard Lamb and let him in here to rest. He's old and he's hurt and I feed him and let him rest. If you keep him out there in irons, you maybe kill him. Also, you get him off at Fort Shaw—tell army chiefs he done nothing. That book you got shows that. You show the book to army chiefs and tell lots of good things about this post. You do that and I'll tell you lots and lots about me and Lamb and Siksika and post here."

Peter considered a moment. The irons he might manage. Getting Lamb into here he might manage too—probably a good idea anyway. The other . . . getting him off . . . not a chance.

"I'll do it. You answer everything I ask about, and I'll make the trade. I'll do you a big favor. I've got lots of influence with the captain chief because he's my brother. It's a good trade, but you'll get more from me than I'll get from you. You'll be ahead, I'm afraid." He smiled.

"Take off irons and bring him here?"

"Yes."

"Get him off at Fort Shaw? Get him free? Tell chiefs there nothing wrong?"

"Yes, of course. Perfectly simple." He smiled agreeably, exuberantly.

"Horseapples," she said.

"Uh, what?"

"You full of horseapples, big-time newspaperman. He'll stay in trouble at Fort Shaw because army runs it, and you not telling army what to do. You not telling your brother what to do. You think I'm dumb Injun, don't you? Pretty dumb. You be big cheese. Hokay, you go get irons off Richard Lamb, and maybe I talk a little anyway."

He considered. He didn't really want to confront Joseph. Not by-the-book Joe, who'd regard Peter's request as interference with army affairs.

"Later," he said. "Let me get my story first and then I'll see about the irons."

She leered, knowingly, and he reddened. He didn't like the way she had put him on the spot. He'd fix her wagon, too.

She smiled triumphantly. "I'll tell you anyway, newspaperman. Ask your questions. I'll tell you about here, and my husband, and the Blackfeet . . . and then you'll owe me something, yes? Owe a lot, yes?"

He was surprised. "Yes, surely, anything you ask," he replied, with a certain inner amusement. What could anyone owe a squaw? "What tribes trade here?"

"Blackfeet and Crow," she said. "Sometimes

Shoshone and Flathead. All friendlies to white man. This is Blackfeet land, belongs to us. Here down to Elk River, what you call Yellowstone. Then they made treaty, in what you say 1855, and made the Musselshell the edge of the Blackfeet land. Then, 1873 they move it north of the Missouri. Then, 1874 further north than that. Pretty soon they take it all. But this still Blackfeet land. The Crow say no, it is their land, but they lose scalps that way."

"No Sioux? Cheyenne?"

She glared. "They enemies, dogs. Unclean. We trade maybe once, twice, but they don't like it here. They trade down on Yellowstone, out on prairie where Yellowstone and Missouri come together, Fort Union. They no good, fight white man, fight us."

He frowned. This wasn't going in the direction he had hoped.

"You sell lots of guns?"

"No, not lots. Traders at Fort Benton and Fort Conrad sell more guns. Almost every Siksika man has gun to shoot the buffalo, fight Crow, and steal horses with. Old guns. They can't afford new guns that shoot many bullets fast. New guns with brass cartridges. Siksika men shoot flintlocks, caplocks, old Norwester smoothbores—that's Hudson Bay gun. Blackfeet trade always with Hudson Bay Company and Canada traders. Much more than Yankee traders. Look for yourself in the book. We sell few old guns, maybe some powder, maybe some lead."

"I will look," he said. "If you don't sell many guns, how do you make a profit?"

"Whiskey." She seemed to remember something. "I mean, we don't sell whiskey, but other traders, Fort Benton, Fort Conrad, they sell lots of whiskey for pelts."

"Maybe more happens here than goes into this book, eh?"

"You bet, newspaperman. We got hundreds of cattle for the miners, and lots of potato and onion and hay for the mining camps, hey? That's in another book. You want it too?"

"Maybe later. Why'd Lamb—why'd your man take up with Blackfeet?"

"He was mountain man, see? Trapper. Lived alone out in mountains. Got lonely and wanted wife, fix his meals and keep nice lodge. Talk to at night beside fire. Besides, I was plenty good-looking then. Everyone say so. Still not bad, hey?"

She grinned. He frowned. He wasn't getting the thing he wanted, the evidence of gun-running. She was too smart. She wasn't admitting to anything of that sort. But he'd trap her eventually. Got her to admit to whiskey, which wasn't legal. He'd work on her more. If worse came to worse, he'd write the story anyway. He knew how to write one that ran on speculation and ducked the hard facts. There was no way he'd give up the best story of his life.

She seemed amused. It irked him that she seemed to be toying with him.

"Why you? Why did he like Blackfeet better than his own kind? Does he hate his own kind?"

She laughed. "He says white women no good in the robes. Say they all stiff as a board. He says Siksika women know how to love a man."

He was nonplussed. It was a thing never discussed in New York.

"Anyway he take people one at a time. Doesn't think of me as Siksika, just as wife. He made his daughters learn to read and write like white man, and I make them keep lodges, like Siksika."

"He's educated . . . I mean, he's good at reading the booksigns, and writing on paper, and ciphering?"

"Sure, newspaperman, he was big teacher, professor at some place called Amherst. He taught boys about very old times across the water. He tell us big stories like our Blackfeet stories— gods on mountains, always crazy up there and torturing people."

Peter was startled. "How'd he end up here? Some dishonor? Broken heart back there?"

"Hell no, newspaperman. He come west because Amherst dull as hell. No buffalo to shoot. People dried up as hard as jerky. He say he come here to come alive. Blackfeet lands, shining mountains, and big sky, made him come alive, see?"

"No I don't, really. There must be other reasons. Things he probably never told you. He must have been in trouble . . ."

"Hah! You don't know Richard Lamb!"

"You mentioned daughters. I met one. You have another?"

"Two daughters, both beautiful. Blackfeet and white blood mix up and make beautiful, and they make men's eyes follow. Twin daughters, and I had hell of a time."

"Where's the other?"

"How do I know? I'm locked in here, big fat guard at the door."

"Tell me, have you sons? Do you and Lamb have a son, maybe a son out trading with other tribes?"

"No. No one else. I'm done talking now. You hungry? Richard Lamb, he always feeds the hungry. No one goes away from here hungry, not even filthy Crow. We feed them, shoot them later. Everyone loves Richard Lamb. He's good man, and lives by laws of white man God."

"I thought he rejected—"

"Naw. He keep that. He says he's free man, long as keep that in his chest." She stood, dismissing him. "Now you owe me lots," she said. "You go get him out of chains and bring him here for feeding like you promised."

He was miffed. He resented being dismissed like some lackey by an old squaw.

"Thank you," he said tightly, and barged out. Back at the bivouac, he settled in some shade and studied the ledger. He found that since the first of the year, Lamb had traded for seventeen guns—six of them old Hudson Bay fusils, one Hawken, two Sharps, several old Springfields, and one Kentucky longrifle. And not a modern weapon on the books. He frowned. He would write the story anyway because it was too good to pass by. He would merely have to use a little more care, and speculate rather than report. He'd done it many times.

June 17, UPPER MUSSELSHELL, Montana Territory: June 17. By special correspondence. Captain Joseph Partridge, based at Fort Shaw, M.T., today uncovered evidence that a renegade white trader named Richard Lamb, now under arrest, was a major provisioner of arms used by hostile plains Indians to massacre the Seventh Cavalry command of Colonel George Custer a year ago.

Captain Partridge was accompanied by his brother, *New York Herald* correspondent Peter Partridge. They believe they may have uncovered a nefarious traffic of arms to red savages that had emboldened Sioux and Cheyenne war factions to strike down Colonel

Custer at the Little Big Horn, thus embarrassing the Republic during its Centennial Celebration.

Trading post ledgers reveal a steady sale of arms to local tribesmen, along with quantities of powder and lead. These sales are recorded in trading post ledgers as having been made to local tribes, but the Partridges believe they are the visible portion of a bloody traffic of arms to hostiles east of the post. Lamb is a peculiarly rich man, with vast herds of cattle and scores of savage retainers who slave in his fields. Such wealth, the Partridges believe, could only have come from the lucrative arms traffic.

Lamb is being held in irons, and questioning by military authorities will begin shortly at Fort Shaw. It is expected that Lamb, an educated renegade, will be convicted, and the mystery of the Little Big Horn will be solved once and for all. And a tragedy still wracking the Northwest and costing the government heavy expenditures can be laid to one man's insatiable greed and contempt for his own people.

Lamb admits to nothing but the evidence is there to confront him.

# CHAPTER 7

He could not sleep. The manacles bit into his wrists, unbalanced him, and destroyed comfort. The cold night air sucked his warmth away and left him cold in the belly. They had not offered him a robe or a blanket. And on top of that, worry churned his mind. What would be their fate? How was Aspen? Black Wolf? The others? What could he do?

A quarter-moon sank and disappeared behind the dark bulk of the Crazies. The sky was not completely overcast, but black cloudmasses were obscuring the stars here and there. When a cloud was overhead the night was very black.

Around him lay the troopers in their bedrolls, turning restlessly on the hard ground, perhaps flicking away ants and spiders and soft things just as he was. A little beyond, in a canvas shelter, lay Captain Partridge and his brother. Lamb wondered whether the New Yorker wore his knickerbockers to bed.

There were four guards, two at the troop's horse herd a hundred yards to the east, and two at the trading post holding Aspen in and the world out. And beyond that, up Elk Creek two hundred yards or so were the lodges, whose smoke sometimes reached him in the moist night air. It would not be long until dawn and then perhaps some fire-warmth, and eventually sun-warmth, which his body cried for the most. He was more tired than he could ever remember being.

The night turned blacker, and there seemed to be a silent bulk over him, and then a warm rough hand on his own. He knew, without seeing, that it was one of his sons-in-law, Standing Bear or Turtle, come down from the hills.

The hand bid him rise. He dared not; the chain would clank. He wondered, too, if there was any sense in it. Should he leave, become a fugitive from the army? He decided he would. He might be old but he would be young enough to take risks and not play it old-man safe. Years in the mountains had taught him the value of calculated risk.

He lifted the warm hand and placed it on his manacle chain. Then he drew his hands apart, stretching the chain so it would not clank. The warm hand understood and soon there were two warm hands lifting him to his feet while he kept the chain taut between his wrists.

They padded on moccasined feet toward the creek and the even deeper gloom of the cotton-woods. He walked awkwardly, his arms straining the chain into taut silence. A soldier coughed in the night and rolled over. A stick snapped like a gunshot beneath his foot, and they froze.

Along the creek bank they walked with greater

ease, the soft noise of their passage masked by the laughing water, and the sight of them obscured by deep shadow. His night vision was no longer keen and his eye watered. But the young man with the warm hands knew that, and a warm hand had clasped the old man's cold one. They passed the trading post, where Aspen slept warm, without incident. At the lodges they paused. Here was another shadowy man, another son-in-law. But there was no one else in sight. Swiftly the two young men added wood to the fires smoldering in the lodges, and threw bones to the curs, who wandered restlessly around the camp.

The old man smelled the pungent smoke of green wood and then he knew. There was no one else here. Every last one of his people had vanished in the night. This wood, some of it green, would give the smoking teepees the appearance of a live village well into the morning, delaying discovery of their escape.

"There is nothing here but the lodges," whispered a voice he knew was Turtle's. "We have cached our things in the mountains and are travelling light. We have the whole horse herd. . . . Luke Old Coyote drifted them all from here to us right under the eyes of the bluecoats and then he told us what was happening here and what the bluecoats intend for us. I am sorry you have been hurt. We would rather die than let them take us north to starve."

That last, the freedom-cry of his son-in-law, weighed heavily on Richard Lamb's heart.

They turned abruptly west, splashed through the creek, soaking their moccasins, and then clambered up a steep slope. The old man's heart beat hard, and his irons unbalanced him. Warm hands helped him over a cutbank curve and then they were padding up a long coulee that was choked with red willow brush along its crease. Beyond a dark ridge there were horses held by Luke Old Coyote. One of them, even in the gloom of the night, seemed to glow dimly and the old man recognized his medicine horse, the great white stallion splashed with black stars, ridden only for the most sacred and solemn ceremonies of his kin.

He stared at the horse, understanding its message. He was to be their leader, old as he was. They would all follow him and depend on him for safety and succor. His white man medicine would enable them to deal with the bluecoats and lead them to some sort of safety, and perhaps back to Eden. He sighed in the night and accepted it. He had not survived as a mountain man by fleeing the hard things.

He could not mount with manacled wrists, but his sons-in-law lifted him astride and handed him plaited reins that led forward to a hackamore over the stallion's nose. He shivered and it was noticed, and a blanket was brought to him. He clutched it awkwardly, one manacled hand on the reins, the other drawing the woolen warmth over his frail shoulders.

And then they were off, bearing southwest and uphill steadily. They were leaving a trail, of course, along with the trail of the whole clan, a trail easily followed even by infantrymen without a guide. He huddled gratefully into the blanket and felt less chilled. His mind was awhirl, weighing options, discarding possibilities. He saw nothing very promising in the hours and days ahead.

Turtle and Standing Bear had done well, he thought. How tempted they must have been to try a classic Blackfeet horse raid, drive off the soldiers' ponies, take a few scalp, free prisoners. If the soldiers had been Crow it would have happened. But they had done this with an eye to the future, an eye toward pacific relations with the whites once again, and had left the soldiers unharmed and the horses untouched. But even as these thoughts coursed through his head, he knew that the brothers Partridge would be no less enraged by Blackfeet temperance than by Blackfeet war. It would make no difference to them whether the Blackfeet abducted an old man, or whether they stole horses and slaughtered half the command. That was the nature of pride: to consider a slight offense as abominable as a great one. He knew that the brothers would howl for revenge soon enough, and that the newsman would seek blood and war and death.

Three hours later, as a false dawn grayed the crags of the mountains, they penetrated the throat of a defile that led into an alpine meadow criss-crossed with rills and bordered with aspen and lodgepole pine that were silhouetted against the high gray cliffs. The others were there. He greeted them solemnly.

Loving hands helped him off the medicine horse. Hope, her eyes alight with reunion, hugged him.

"I am glad you're safe," she whispered. "And how is mother?"

"Safe in the house . . . for now," he said, suddenly unsure of the truth of it. "And caring for Black Wolf, who will be a long time in his robes."

Faith, too, was there, her bright blue eyes peering into his old and watery one. She welcomed him silently with a smile and a warning. "The most dangerous of them is the newspaperman. I had a difficult time with him . . . no, he did nothing to me but threaten. But he is the key to everything. Soldiers, we can understand; but that man . . . I cannot understand at all. I see evil in him, Father."

It was an interesting insight, he thought. He smelled meat cooking and knew he was famished, but they led him instead to a flat boulder and bade him rest his manacled wrist there just so, with the riveted brass lock that would free the hinged cuff resting on the rock. Many miles away, Captain Partridge had the square key. Turtle placed the blade of a trade hatchet into the mechanism, and tapped deftly with the butt of another trade hatchet until the cuff sprang free. In another moment the second cuff was opened, and the old man rubbed his raw wrists with hands that were once again his own.

His lovely Faith was at his side again, this time with a salve of wool fat, a creamy balm she rubbed into his stinging red flesh. After applying it liberally she bound each raw wrist with a strip of calico, and then kissed his bearded and blood-encrusted cheek. With that, some pemmican, and some rest he'd be fine, he thought. But they had stopped here for a hot meal instead of pemmican, and he sensed it was for him. In flight, the Blackfeet rarely stopped for anything, and left their weak ones behind them. In a little while he would feel whole.

But there was no time. The soldiers would be after them soon. This camp was only three hours from the trading post and there was a clear trail, made by thirty ponies, pointing the way.

He ate silently and with appetite he didn't know he still had. The trembling of his legs had ceased and warmth radiated from his belly out upon his numb fingers.

They were waiting for him to lead them—somewhere. To make decisions of some kind. He wanted time to think, but there was none.

Slowly he surveyed this camp. The young men guarded the throat of the valley with Henry repeaters he had given them years ago for the protection of the trading post. With those, they could hold off a formidable army. The five Henrys were carried by his sons-in-law, the two brothers of Standing Bear, and a nephew of Aspen. His own was back in the bivouac, in Captain Partridge's hands, and could be turned against them here if the army found ammunition for it.

Against them was a detail of mounted infantry with single-shot Springfields that had far greater range than the Henrys but were slower to load and fire. He sighed. War was the last thing he wanted, the one thing that would brand this village as hostiles and bring down General Crook's or General Howard's column.

Up on the grasses were the ponies, looking fat and rested and being watched diligently by young Luke, who had an old single-shot carbine crooked in his arm.

Wrapped in a fine buffalo robe were Grandfather Singing Bird and Grandmother Prairie Dog Song. They looked weary after only three hours of travel, and Lamb wondered how soon he'd be building a scaffold in the crotch of a cottonwood tree for the old people on their way to the Sand-hills.

There were no travois. They had left the lodges with loaded travois in the night, had cached most of their possessions somewhere, and now were travelling as lightly as hunting and war parties. With some of the children riding double there were enough ponies, but none to spare. A single lame horse would bring trouble.

Twenty-four souls here, some very young or very old, plus two more back at the trading post on Elk Creek, and all of them waiting for him to lead them to safety and make medicine and miracles. He sighed. He was no Moses, and they were fleeing the Promised Land, not seeking it.

And what would Captain Partridge do? he wondered. Joseph Partridge, the aristocrat? Send for help, no doubt. Send a dispatch rider to Fort Ellis near Three Forks, and within a day or two the bluecoats would swarm over central Montana hunting these runaways . . . with orders to kill.

A thought troubled him: Would they threaten Aspen? Use Aspen in some way as a lever? The newsman would. Whether his stolid rule-book brother would, he wasn't sure.

Richard Lamb sighed, knowing what he would do and not liking it at all. He would take his kin as swiftly as possible north to the reservation lands above the Missouri. Fast, before they were declared fugitives and ambushed and slaughtered by roving army patrols. Fast, before Partridge caught them. Fast, to draw Partridge away from Aspen and the trading post. At the reservation there would be help and friends.

There were two ways. The long one would take them northeast, through Judith Gap between the Snowy Mountains and the Little Belt Mountains, and up past Fort Benton and across the Missouri. But that route would take them back toward the trading post and Partridge's squad.

The other was to push up the Musselshell, head west until they hit the Smith River basin, and follow it north through rugged mountains. It was shorter and ran straight toward the reservation. But his kin would have to duck around Camp Baker, which lay west of the Smith River, and was garrisoned by a handful of soldiers protecting nearby mining camps. And, after that, they would have to bypass Fort Shaw itself. But if they could slip past the soldiers, they could make it to the Indian Agency on Badger Creek where they could report, and the army would leave them alone.

His mind grew firm on it. The very act of heading for the reservation made them friendlies. It was safety for his people, visible compliance, and no doubt, in time, a chance to return to the trading post after the Indian wars were over. But would his kin accept that?

As for the charges against him, he supposed they would vanish once he delivered his kin to the reservation. In any case, he knew, the army had no jurisdiction over him. A military tribunal could not sentence him to a military stockade, at least not in normal times. They could go to a federal court and bring charges through a U.S. Attorney if they wished. But those niceties could vanish in a time of war, and it was true that the military ran the territories until they acquired statehood. Anything could happen to him, depending on the whims of Crook or Terry or Howard or Gibbon. Not that it mattered: The West was a vast and unexplored place, and he and Aspen could vanish for a while. He knew every mountain man trail and refuge in the Northwest, and would use them if he must.

His mind made up, he gathered his kin to him and explained his intention amid dark stares. It did not sit well with them, especially the young men, that they should end up doing exactly what the bluecoats demanded. If they had wanted that, why had they fled, left lodges behind?

"But Father," protested Turtle. "Why must we run like a buffalo calf from the wolves? We have Henrys. We are more than a match for the blue-coats."

Lamb gazed fondly at his son-in-law and at the bright woman beside him, his daughter Hope, and the image filled his mind of Turtle lying lifeless and bloody, and of Hope being led away by soldiers to a shameful fate. He felt weak and old.

"There are four great columns of bluecoats near us," he began softly. "Howard to the west, Gibbon, Crook, and Terry to the south and east. More bluecoats than one can count, and with cannon and the talking wires to tell them where we are."

Turtle swelled with emotion. "Then let us die bravely here!" he cried.

"Father Sun has abandoned the Siksika people, so let us fight and die!" cried Coyote Runs, a brother of Standing Bear.

Lamb tried again. "In a few moons, when the Cold Maker comes, these wars will be over and we will return to Elk Creek. Bad times pass. Father Sun has not abandoned you; there is only a cloud hiding him."

"We will starve. The buffalo are nearly gone and the agent there cheats the people."

"I have a trader friend at Fort Conrad. You know his wife, Na-tak-i, a Piegan. They will supply us. I will pay him."

"But the bluecoats will take you away."

"That will come to nothing," Lamb replied. "We must run a race now and be there before the talking wires tell of us and the soldiers swarm after us. We will go up the Smith River—it is shortest and will be easiest for the old ones. We will slip at night around Camp Baker, and, again, we will slip around Fort Shaw, and then report to the new agency on Badger Creek. Then we will be safe. On the reservation, we can travel in peace to Fort Conrad where I will arrange for lodges and food with our friends there. But we must hurry. We are only three hours from Elk Creek and the captain, and we have left a wide trail."

It was decided then. No one objected. His medicine was their medicine. He turned and stared at the awesome gray peaks to the south and west. They could flee to safety up there—at least for a while. But he preferred to reach the reservation.

The fate of Aspen and Black Wolf worried him. If he took this band to the Indian Agency and reported there, the soldiers would probably bring Aspen and Black Wolf up there too and that would end the trouble. That was Partridge's mission, after all. They would be reunited at the agency, or up at the trading post on the Marias River that was run by his friends Berry and Shultz. They would have a good camp through the long summer, hunt buffalo, pick berries in the moon of sarvis berries, and make pemmican for winter. The Marias country was sunlit prairie, and the summer captivity would pass without pain. It pleased him, for there was no month and no place in all of the universe like a warm and sunny September on the high plains of the Piegan Blackfeet country. He was no longer weary, but eager with anticipation. Around him, the ponies were being swiftly hackamored and loaded. Grandfather Singing Bird and Grandmother Prairie Dog Song were mounted, and a young man was lashing their buffalo robes behind them.

Then Standing Bear, at the throat of the defile, raised an arm and cried out, "Someone comes."

A swift silence enveloped the band. In the quiet, Richard Lamb steered his great white medicine horse toward the defile and stared down the long sloping meadows to a line of black fir trees far below. His old eye picked up movement there, but he could not make out what it was. "Tell me," he asked brusquely.

"A man on a horse riding this way," Standing Bear replied.

They waited in the dawn sun.

"He is a bluecoat," said Standing Bear at last. The other young men were present now, checking their Henrys, checking their pouches of .44 cartridges.

"Do not shoot," said Lamb sharply. "It could mean the end of us all."

The horseman below picked his way along the broad trail of bent and trampled grasses that led directly to the defile. He paused and saw them there at the mouth of the rock, and from his kit he drew a white rag and tied it to the blade of his officer's saber. Then he walked his bay army mount slowly up the long slope, the saber pointed straight in the sky.

Richard Lamb saw the shine of the captain's bars on the bluecoated shoulders, and made out the stern face of Captain Joseph Partridge.

# CHAPTER 8

Captain Partridge had awakened at false dawn.
Light did that to him, especially out on bivouac
when he slept poorly. He peered out of his canvas
shelter into the gray murk of a new day and
stepped out. It was not yet five and he had set
reveille at six and hoped to be off to Fort Shaw
with the Indians and Lamb by seven or eight.

He could not see the lodges in the gray gloom
but he smelled the smoke of them. Off in the
meadow to the east were his army horses, and
one of his guards was visible riding among them.
He saw too the guard at the trading post door. It
was very quiet, except for the occasional trill of
the early birds. There was a heavy dew, and he
was glad he had slept under a shelter half.

There would be dew on the bedrolls of his men.
Lamb had no bedroll and was no doubt chilled,
but it didn't matter. He'd warm up at the breakfast fire soon enough. But Lamb wasn't there.
Partridge peered at the sleeping forms one by
one, and found no bearded old man among them.
Gone to the bushes, he thought, and strode easily
to the cottonwoods along the creek. No Lamb.
No Lamb either near the horses, or at the out-
house of the trading post.

Perhaps inside the post itself. He barged past the

guard at the door and into the gloomy building and stared. The buck, Black Wolf, wheezed in his blankets on the floor of the trading room. The squaw, Aspen, stared darkly at him from under her robes when he entered the bedroom. No Lamb.

Uneasily he trotted to the lodges up the creek. The mutts were there, sidling uneasily from him. Smoke curled from several teepees. But it was all wrong, desperately wrong. Life was missing. The thin-sliced meat, drying into jerky on the racks, was gone. The parfleches had vanished. The totem-laden tripod with its grisly scalps had disappeared. He peered into one of the canvas teepees, knowing what he would find, and then into the other lodges, one by one. They were gone, every last one of them. And so was Lamb. But they had not been gone long because the fires still smoldered. Two, three hours at the most, he surmised.

Gone! Hostiles! He paused at the edge of the circle of lodges. Go after them? It could mean a fight. They were no doubt armed. In fact, Lamb had said as much. But with what? Old caplocks?

They could be caught easily. There would be a trail so fresh and visible that a pilgrim could follow it. And they couldn't go fast, not with those teeming children and the old ones. . . .

Get help, that would be important, and the proper army procedure, too. Murphy knew this country, he would send him. Fort Ellis would be a hundred miles closer than Fort Shaw, maybe a hundred miles from here, figuring a detour around the Crazy Mountains. Ellis could wire Shaw, or maybe send patrols out. Joseph hated to send out a dispatch; it was an admission of defeat, the botching of a simple job. It'd look bad. He'd been assigned to round up a few ancient and friendly Piegans, and a few children, and deliver them to their reservation, only to have them squirt away and turn hostile. If only Peter hadn't pushed him so hard, made him throw his weight around chasing glory. . . .

It irked him. There had been army experience to follow, army wisdom, the fruit of dealing for decades with savages, and his brother had paid no heed to it and had relentlessly badgered him toward war and blood and glory.

Peeved, he stormed back to the bivouac and shook Private Pinski awake. "Call reveille," he grated. "On the double, on the double!"

Pinski, in red long johns, rolled out, found the cold brass trumpet laden with dew, blew sour notes until the brass warmed to his breath, and awakened them all with dissonant honking. The last notes vanished eerily into the thick predawn air. Peter Partridge stared from under the shelter.

"I want you all dressed, packed, and saddled in fifteen minutes," the captain barked. "The Piegans are gone and Lamb with them. Slipped out two or three hours ago, lodge-fires still burning. We're going after them—they can't be far ahead. They've loaded up everything, all their gear. They've got children and old ones. Draw hardtack, we're not waiting around for mess. Assemble here."

Men stared at him a moment, and then scurried to work, rolling bedrolls, jamming on boots.

"Murphy!" the captain cried. "Over here."

"Sor?"

"You know this country. I'm dispatching a message to Ellis. It's maybe a hundred miles closer than Shaw. You'll draw rations and take a second mount, one of the pack mules. I want you at Fort Ellis within forty-eight hours. Now tell me how you'll get there."

"Why, Sor, south around the Crazies, starting westward. To the Shields River valley, and then the Yellerstone, and up Bozeman Pass, Sor. And she's on the left at the top, comin' into the Gallatin valley."

"That's fine, Private. I'll have a dispatch for you in a moment. The CO may choose to send patrols or he may wire Shaw, or both. He may have instructions for me that he will send back with you. Understand?"

"Yes, Sor. And where will you be when I meet yourself, Sor?"

He hadn't thought of that. "Here," he said. "Or if not, I'll leave word inside the post, and you can follow. Understand?"

"Yes, Sor."

Peter approached, suddenly alive. "Joe, does Ellis have a wire?"

"Yes, why?"

"I'd like to send my dispatches to New York. Can the private take them?"

"Don't see why not."

"I'll have them telegraphed to the *Herald* collect. Can that be done?"

"I imagine, but not if it interferes with military traffic."

Peter was exuberant. He'd get his stories back to New York a lot faster than he had imagined.

"I'll have them in a moment, Private," he shouted. "Have them wired collect, understand? And report to me when you get back whether they were sent or not."

He raced to the shelter, extracted his two dispatches, scribbled instructions on them, and watched ecstatically as Murphy tucked them into his saddle kit.

The captain was hastily assembling his kit when Peter returned with a question: "Who's going to guard that squaw and that injured buck at the post while we're gone?"

"Hadn't thought of it," Joseph muttered. He would have to post two guards who could relieve each other. Or take the squaw with them and leave the buck to fend for himself. The injured Indian wasn't going anywhere anyway.

He decided on the guards. There was property here to be guarded. He didn't want his CO to find even more reasons to pin his ears back. Colonel Ambrose was a martinet who second-guessed all of his officers—and usually was right.

Partridge walked over to the pair who were still posted at the doors.

"Fiske, Johnson, you're staying here guarding these army prisoners. Don't let her out except for necessary purposes. You're responsible for the property here as well. Lose her, or lose property, and you'll be in trouble from here to Washington, D.C." That sounded too rough. He smiled. "Easy duty. No bullets or hard rides. Enjoy yourselves. I'll send orders if we don't return directly."

They grinned at him.

That left him with seven men, plus Peter and himself. Enough to herd a few Piegan women and children, even if they had a rifle or two.

Peter was jubilant as they jointly folded up the canvas shelter and loaded up gear. "They're hostiles now. You can shoot the bastards if they resist, get that old renegade, make a name with some swift action—"

Joseph glared at him coldly. "It is not my mission or the army's to take civilian lives," he replied tersely.

Peter was unrebuked. "You've got hostages. Tell Lamb you'll shoot the old squaw. The old man's gone on her anyway. He'll just trot on back here, him and those savages. You just tell him it's the firing squad for her and the injured buck unless the band returns."

Joseph stared at his brother. In truth, he had never thought of that. It might be better than chasing after the band, and risking possible bloodshed if they resisted; blood of those squaws and children . . . possible army inquiries, the public in an uproar . . . an officer in trouble. . . . He'd seen it all; seen the public howl after the Baker massacre, Washita, Sand Creek. . . . This way would be bloodless.

"Peter!" he exclaimed. "You've given me an idea. I'm going after them alone."

"But—"

"This is a bloodless mission and it's going to stay bloodless. That hostage idea will work just fine. Lamb'll turn that band around the moment he discovers his squaw isn't as safe as he thinks."

Peter looked angry, wanted to tell the army—his brother—how to do it. Wanting to report to the *Herald* a small triumphant battle led by Joseph. But he swallowed his rage. He knew it was futile to push Joseph too far, especially on army matters.

The captain walked over to the bugler. "Pinski, give me a tune. I want to address the men."

In a moment they were gathered.

"You're not going," he announced. "I've got a better plan. I'm going alone. Corporal Rudeen, you'll be in charge and responsible to me alone.

Protect this post and guard the prisoners and run an orderly camp. Make meat if you wish, but keep your hunters close at hand for swift deployment. If any trading parties or tribesmen come, turn them away. If I am not back by dark, come after me at first light tomorrow. I will be following the trail of the band, and you can hardly miss it. Are there any questions?"

"I'm going with you," said Peter.

The captain considered. "I'm afraid not," he replied slowly.

"You can't stop me, Joe; I'm a civilian."

The captain sighed. A public quarrel in front of his men.

"If you do, it'll be on foot. Corporal Rudeen, this is a direct order: All army mounts are to be kept here under guard. The two trading post horses we harnessed yesterday are to be kept here as well. Don't fail me."

"Yessir," said the tall, blond corporal.

"Sorry, Peter." It was a hard thing to do but necessary. Through this whole mission he'd been pressured and unbalanced by his younger brother's importuning, and it had gotten him into trouble. Everything from Peter's potshot that had almost killed Lamb, onward.

Peter reddened and stalked off toward the abandoned lodges.

"Return to your duties, and have yourselves a hot mess," the captain said.

"Sir?" asked Corporal Rudeen. "I don't quite understand. Begging your pardon, Sir, but could you tell me why you're going alone?"

Captain Partridge did so, and saddled up his bay with the split-seat McClellan cavalry saddle he had been issued. By his turnip watch, it was still barely five. False dawn must have come soon after four in this latitude, at this time of year. He splashed west across Elk Creek and found the broad trail he knew would be there, with long scrapes of travois poles pointing the way like arrows into the high Crazy Mountains. The occasional horse piles were fresh and green and not dried in the slightest. The trail took him around and over towering foothill ridges and mounds, small mountains in themselves, topped by black ponderosa or juniper. An hour or so later, he noticed that the travois marks had vanished and he wondered about it. They had lightened their load or divided or gotten more ponies, he supposed. He hoped they hadn't scattered. That would ruin everything.

After another hour, in which the sun finally rose and shone pinkly upon the great gray pillars of rock ahead, he watered his horse at a creek and noted that the trail, if anything, was fresher still. He swore he could smell the acrid scent of horse in the grasses. He let the bay rest a few minutes— it had been a steady uphill climb from Elk Creek. The bay snorted and began nipping seed heads from wild timothy grass. Then, impatiently, he mounted the sidestepping bay again and pushed on up the trail which led directly toward a great declivity ahead. At a treeline he pulled his glass from his kit and studied that gateway of rock. The glass settled upon the figure of a man, and then another, with black sticks cradled in their arms, and his heart began to pound. Men with rifles. It raised a turmoil in his gut. He realized he was hungry. He'd been so intent upon the trail that he had forgotten to munch the hardtack he had packed.

From his kit he extracted a white linen under-shirt and tied it to the blade of his saber with thong, tightly enough so that it would not slip. Then he raised the saber and kicked the bay forward. As he drew closer, one of the small figures vanished. Good. Word would reach Lamb. Then there were four men—he could identify them as Indians now—all armed, all watching his progress from the mouth of the defile. He approached to about fifty or sixty yards and halted. It was far enough. If they planned to shoot those Henrys—he was a little surprised to see those fine repeaters here—he'd have a pretty good chance to wheel out of there. He did not have to wait long.

The old man appeared then, astride a peculiar white-spotted mount. It was Lamb, all right. Unarmed, it seemed, his hands free of manacles and his wrists bound in bright cloth. Behind him, also on ponies, were two young men the captain had never seen—Lamb's sons-in-law, no doubt. Each was carrying a Henry, its brass frame glinting in the long early sun.

For an instant he thought he might simply kidnap the old man and leave this band leaderless. But he knew even as he considered it that that was not his mission, and if he tried it he would die fast.

"Well, boy, ye've come to palaver, have ye?"

"Mr. Lamb, I have indeed, and what I have to say will take barely a minute. Unless you and your Piegans are back at your trading post by dawn tomorrow, your squaw and her brother will be executed by firing squad. You are hostiles now, and the whole army will soon be after you —unless you turn around."

He smiled grimly.

The old man's eye bored into him like a blue cannon muzzle, but he said nothing. Partridge could not escape the feeling that there was something majestic in that old man and his glare.

But he congratulated himself that it was really the stare of a helpless adversary. He was doing this the army way, the way countless soldiers had learned to deal with savages over many years. He was giving Lamb some time; time to go back to his people, sit and talk, and come around to the inevitable. Back up that valley, an elder would tamp tobacco into the red pipestone bowl of his long medicine pipe, honor the cardinal directions and the earth and sky, puff, and pass the pipe to the others in council. Then they would gravely discuss the options, and conclude that they must do what they must do, and go back to Elk Creek. The army and Joseph Partridge understood ceremony, even if Peter did not. If Peter had been here, Joseph thought, he would be urging bugles and bullets upon his brother. And many would die, including, perhaps, Peter and himself. No. These savages, and Lamb too, were free men, and should be led to decisions instead of forced to them.

"Ye'd kill an innocent woman, would ye?" Lamb asked. "What is her crime, I ask ye?"

"No crime whatsoever, as far as I know," Joseph replied. "She has the misfortune of being a hostage."

"Ye'd shoot her for nothing, then, ye'd shoot her for naught."

"Her blood would be upon your hands, Lamb, not mine. You return with these Piegans before dawn, and she's safe. Her execution is up to you, not me."

"That reasoning's a little peculiar," replied Lamb. "Ye'd give the command to shoot, I imagine."

"Only if you trigger it with disobedience of the army."

"And Black Wolf too, eh? What's his crime, eh?"

"He has the misfortune of being a hostage also. Quite apart from his defiance of us. Hostages are levers, Lamb. And I am pulling the lever that will bring you in with the least possible bloodshed."

"Least blood, is it? And when these people are thrown upon the mercy of the Indian Agent, and starve and sicken and die up there on Badger Creek, will ye still believe there is no blood upon ye, to ye'r way of thinking?"

"I am under orders to—"

"Yes, yes, I know. So ye'd shoot an innocent woman in cold blood, eh? I'll not soon forget it. Go on back now. Ye've delivered ye'r bloody message. I'll talk it over with my kin. And these murderin' savages will come to some kind of decision. Eh?"

"I'm not done talking with you yet," the captain retorted coldly. He didn't like being dismissed. "I've sent a dispatch to Fort Ellis. You've no place to go. South, east, west, soldiers will be swarming over you. Howard's over west, corralling the Nez Percé. Miles and Crook are south and east. From the north, patrols from Fort Shaw will find any needle in any haystack in central Montana. Think about it."

"Very impressive, Captain. We'll think about it. Some will appeal to Father Sun or the Old Man, as they call God. I don't know whether ye've got one—God, I mean, but ye'd do well to ask Him about shooting innocent women, eh?"

The old man wheeled his proud dappled horse and walked back into the defile while both of his sons-in-law stared at Partridge, unmoving. The captain turned his bay and headed slowly downslope. To hurry would be a sign of fear, even though his back tingled. He'd be back at the Elk Creek bivouac in time for the noon mess.

Strange how the old man talked about God, he thought. As if God had anything to do with it, especially out here. God never paid any attention to affairs west of the Missouri River. Well, why take notice of the rambling of an old man with an eye upon his Maker. That sort of talk wouldn't alter events anyway. If the squaw had to die, she had to die.

He was back at the Elk Creek camp before noon.

"There were at least four Henrys in that band," he told Peter with some relish. "If we'd tried to force the issue we'd have been shot to bits. Including you."

Peter scoffed. "Springfields have more range and more killing power."

"You're right. Custer had them. His scouts had Henrys," Joseph replied.

Peter grinned. "Savages can't aim. Everyone knows that."

Joseph stared, and Peter's eyes gave way.

"At any rate," Joseph said cheerfully, "they'll be back. Expect them around dusk. They'll delay as long as possible, for pride's sake."

"And if they don't come?"

Joseph stared into the big sky. "We'll have to do it. The army never backs down on its threats. If we did, we'd lose our credibility."

"The men will balk."

Joseph replied harshly: "They're soldiers and will do as they're told. There's court-martial and other measures."

"Such as?"

"You, Peter. You've begged for blood this whole trip. You've been our one-man war party. The rest of us have seen combat, you know. Maybe in the morning you'll have a chance to shoot a savage."

# CHAPTER 9

He rode back into the rising valley thinking of death. Not Aspen's death, actually, though that was heavy in his mind, but his own. He had lived too long, into a new era. He had lingered on past the time of his calling, when the land was free and new, and a man felt no boundaries. Now the bluecoated vanguards of schools and farms and stores and brick-paved streets had come, and he could not abide them or what they represented, and would soon die.

He knew what he would do, even as he walked his medicine horse back to the gathering of his kin in the meadow. He would urge them to go to the reservation. He would ride alone back to the trading post and tell Partridge that the Piegans were en route north and would report to the Agency within a fortnight. Then Partridge would take him to Fort Shaw and whatever fate awaited him there—it didn't matter to him for he was dead now—and they'd take Aspen and Black Wolf up to the Agency where their kin was, and that would be the end of it.

There was a council awaiting him, but not the formal council that Captain Partridge had imagined. There were no chiefs or medicine men in this kin-gathering; just himself and the young men, save for Luke Old Coyote who stood sentry at the defile.

"Go swiftly to the reservation," he said abruptly. "If we all go back to Elk Creek they will take away your Henrys. At the reservation you can keep them and perhaps make meat with them and supplement the Agency food, what little there is of it."

"But Father," objected Turtle, "will that save our mother Aspen?"

"I think so. The bluecoat chief will accept my word that you are heading north, and that you will report to the Agency. Then it will all be over." He was not very sure of that.

"We could go back and get our lodges," said Coyote Runs.

"And lose your Henrys. I think as long as you

keep those repeaters you will always be in a position to bargain." He wasn't sure of that, either.

Standing Bear did not like it, and stood up. "Let us free the prisoners rather than surrender like whipped dogs. Let us steal the horses if we can, and while that diverts their attention, free our mother Aspen and Black Wolf. That is the way of the Piegan and of our ancestors. We can spy upon them until late at night, and then make the raid."

"And then what?" asked Lamb.

"The women and children and grandfathers could go to the reservation. Those of us with Henrys could find the great Sioux war chief, Crazy Horse, in the east."

Lamb thought, In scarcely a day the stupid Partridges have managed to turn these friendly people into hostiles.

"The soldier chief will think of the possibility of a raid if we don't show up by dark," Lamb said quietly. "He will prepare—extra guards at the horse herd, and extra guards at the trading post."

Standing Bear pondered that. "But if you go back alone, the soldiers will capture you again and take you to their fort, and your life will be over. And so will that of our mother Aspen, who lives each sun for you."

"I don't expect to die soon," he replied. "What matters now is the future of the young. Somehow, the young must live, and grow strong in a new kind of world."

No one spoke for a while. The rising sun had flooded the mountain meadow with light, and Lamb noticed the spring flowers blooming riotously in patches of azure and purple and yellow and salmon.

"If you leave now, you'll be a day from here before I ride back to the trading post," he said. "And you can strike northwest toward the Musselshell, and then up the Smith River valley. There is no one following you now, and you can travel slowly so that Grandfather and Grandmother can bear the pace. I will stay and rest, leave here when the sun is low, and talk to the soldier chief, Partridge."

They did not like it.

"Be gone!" he cried. "Guard the women and children. Guard my daughters and my grandchildren and my kin!"

Slowly they acquiesced, not because they thought it was right, but because of his patriarchal authority. Something more than medicine; something that told them that Richard Lamb understood the mysterious dark ways of white men, and thus was doing what was best.

Silently they mounted their ponies, wiry mustang horses of dun and black and paint and flaxen-maned sorrel and grulla, staring at the old man. He clasped the hand of Hope in his big rough ones and peered up at her as she sat astride a red roan. And then he clasped the hand of Faith likewise, and muttered, "Godspeed." He wondered if it might be a final parting.

They trotted out of the meadow and veered sharply west and north to angle away from Elk Creek. After two or three hours through rugged foothills they would strike the south fork of the Musselshell, and then race west to the Smith River valley, and then north to the southern reaches of the reservation—and safety, of a sort.

He was alone, save for the great spotted white stallion cropping timothy grass from among the patches of larkspur. The sun was blinding, and its warmth pierced his chilled flesh. His raw wrists hurt within their bandages. He was unarmed. In his saddle kit he knew were things he always kept there—pemmican and jerky and a ball of the soap he had taught Aspen to make from the lye of wood ashes and rendered fat. His appetite had grown small with age, and he needed no food to sustain him now. Much more, he needed to be clean. He extracted the tawny ball of soap.

At the little rill beside the new-leaved aspens he stripped, pulling off his stained buckskin shirt and trousers, and his gray long johns. In the icy water he washed his white hair and then his face—taking care to rinse the caked blood out of his beard—then the rest of himself. And finally he scrubbed patiently on the golden buckskins until the mud and blood and grass stains were gone, or as muted as he could manage. Then he laid the clothing out upon the grasses, knowing how swiftly the sun and the breezes would dry them.

He stood naked in the sun, goose-bumped, waiting for it and the zephyrs to dry him. There was little warmth in it so early in the morning; not the warmth an old man needed. The sun was sacred to his Blackfeet kin, who honored it with a great tribal festival and dance every summer. Now he felt its benevolence touch his pale flesh that had known the elements through a lifetime in the wilderness. He was tired, and later he would spread his saddle blanket in the shade of the tender aspen and sleep. But now he stood naked in the sun, wanting to conduct a small ceremony of surrender, not to the Blackfeet sun deity, but to his own God, whose laws and love he had not forgotten.

"This land is changing," he said aloud to the air, "and I have lived my time in it when it was wild and free and I was a lord of these borders. But that time has passed, and now old Amherst marches in coats of blue and nothing is the same for me, or for my kin.

"I have enjoyed my time. In my footsteps came Aspen, twenty-eight years younger than I, my beautiful daughters, and their little ones. It is time for them to inherit the earth. My own days, what few remain, count for little. If by my passing," said Richard Lamb, "I can preserve what follows in my path, then let me pass. If there is to be a passing, let it be my own. They are not yet ready for the Sandhills."

Thus prayed Lamb. He spread his saddle blanket in shade and dozed through the hot and silent day, knowing contentedly that his kin were slipping farther and farther from the mad Partridges. By the time the sun was far to the west and shadow crept across the alpine grasses, he was rested and the skins were dry. He dressed, and laced tight his fine black moccasins.

He hackamored the stallion and curried the calm animal with handfuls of grass until its coat was smooth and glossy. Then he threw the saddle over and drew up the latigo tight through the cinch ring, kneeing the horse's air from its full lungs. Then he untied its woven buffalo hide hobble, stepped into the stirrups, and set the animal toward Elk Creek, filled with quiet. He had known this quiet many times. The quiet of the heart was the thing he had first found in the West. Now his heart was quiet again, perhaps for the last time. He did not know what he would say when he got to Elk Creek, but that didn't bother him.

He rode into the bivouac at a moment when the soldiers were at evening mess. His arrival had been heralded by a sentinel on the hill, just as the coming of the soldiers had been seen by Bigtooth Beaver from the same outlook. For some mysterious reason the horse knew itself to be a medicine animal, and now as it approached the blueshirted soldiers it was charged with lightning and raced forward with an arched neck and a high tail, a lord carrying a lord.

The old man sat erect, sun streaming through his snowy beard, haloing his white hair, and glinting and glancing upon the sacred beadwork of his buckskins. The sunlight played upon him and his proud horse, scattering fragments that leapt from their flesh, shards of light like a thousand arrows, medicine light, savage strength. The old man did not know that he was an apparition to all that beheld him, including Aspen, who watched from the slit window of the trading post.

The late sunlight caught the blue of the soldiers' shirts and turned it to sapphires. He saw a patch of blue out among the dark-hued army mounts, another splash of blue at the trading post door, and another, with small glints of gold at the epaulets, near the cookfire. And other shadowed blues sat low near the fire, along with a smear of knickered brown.

The old man quieted his horse before the captain and focused his eye upon the face of ambition.

Peter, chewing a slab of venison, stared uneasily, moved by some force he didn't understand.

"Well," said the captain testily, "where are the rest?"

Lamb did not answer for a long moment. Then, "They have surrendered to your wishes and are on their way to the reservation. . . . They will report to the Agency in a few days."

"The reservation? How do I know that?"

"Ye have my word."

"Your word! You didn't keep your word and bring them here."

"I don't recollect giving ye my word."

The captain glared. "You've disobeyed me, Lamb."

The old man, from his mount, considered the accusation. "I don't believe so," he said. "I've sent them to the reservation, exactly as ye wished."

The captain paced furiously. "That wasn't my mission. My orders were to *escort* this band."

The old man grinned slightly. "Ye'r superiors wanted the Indians put on the reservation, eh? I don't suppose the escorting was very important to them, eh?"

"I was ordered to escort them and now they've escaped, thanks to you."

Lamb stared at the obtuse man before him and felt something like pity. He tried again. "I think maybe they'd be commending ye for it. Now ye can return to Fort Shaw and tell them ye did better than they asked."

The captain glowered. "You disobeyed me, and now we'll have to chase them."

Around the bivouac soldiers listened intently as they ate. An unarmed old man on a proud horse was addressing the captain with barely concealed disgust.

"It's too late for that, boy. They have a day's march on ye, and they'll be up there before ye'll catch up."

Peter spoke up: "Forget those Indians, Joe. The thing is, we've got the old renegade back and we can take him up to Fort Shaw for a hearing and all. Gun-running and all the rest."

"Gun-running!" Captain Partridge exploded. "What are you talking about?"

"Why, guns to the hostiles. . . ."

"Peter, you stay out of this. Lamb, the U.S. Army keeps its word. I told you to bring those Blackfeet here or something would happen at dawn. You failed to obey and so something is going to happen at dawn."

The old man grew very still. "I tell ye what," he said quietly. "I'll stand in her place. She's guilty of nothing in ye'r eyes, eh? Ye need no hostage if ye have me, eh? Ye take her to the reservation, and Black Wolf too, eh, and I'll stand in for ye."

There was a sudden hush and they stared at him, half afraid.

"Don't let him cheat you, Joe," cried Peter. "Take him to the fort for his trial and make him watch army discipline first. It'll be a great story."

"That's exactly what I'll do," snarled the captain.

"Cheat ye, eh?" said Lamb. "Ye'll be cheated if I die?" His eye bored into Peter Partridge, who reddened. "Ye have something better than my death in mind, eh?"

It was out then and the soldiers had an inkling of what dawn would bring. They stirred uneasily.

"Tell me, what is this gun-running ye talk of, lad?"

"That should be obvious to you," Peter replied sourly.

"It isn't," said Lamb. "Do ye think it's true?"

Peter shrugged. "What is truth?" he asked.

Aspen, Aspen, he thought. They'll have ye for breakfast. Ye can take one or two with the old caplocks if ye would, but ye won't. I have no way to save ye from this lunatic unless. . . .

From the slit window of the trading post dangled a battered old carbine and a leather pouch. It hung like a black stick, unnoticed. Aspen was arming him from the bedroom cache, if he could reach it. It looked to be a single-shot breech-action. Enough, perhaps. The weapon hung around the corner from the guard at the door.

He turned the horse away from the bivouac and its apoplectic leader, and walked quietly toward the post, his back prickling as he negotiated the hundred or so yards.

"Lamb," roared the captain, "where are you going?"

"To visit my wife," he replied softly.

"I didn't give you permission. Guard, don't let him in!"

The guard held his Springfield at the ready, and blocked the door nervously.

"Will ye not let a man say goodbye?" he called back to the captain. He walked the horse straight toward the guard. Then, when he reached the corner of the post, he swerved right and trotted along its narrow side, plucking the carbine and bag as he passed, his body shielding the act from observers.

"Thank ye, love," he muttered, glimpsing her soft eyes and wetted cheeks in the slitted window.

"You go safe now, Richard Lamb. I love you," said a small strident voice from within.

"I love ye, Aspen," he said, touching his heels to the flanks of the great animal. It bounded into an easy lope upstream, and into the canopied cottonwoods.

"Stop him!" cried Captain Partridge. There were pistol shots now, and the captain and his brother emptied their revolvers at the distant fleeing target. The Springfields had been stacked and were useless for the moment.

No bullet came close. Richard Lamb splashed easily into the creek, over to the west side, and then toward the empty lodges. Behind him on the wind came hoarse cries of soldiers, and then he was beyond hearing. He crossed the creek again quietly and walked into the circle of lodges straight toward that of Grandfather Singing Bird. It had a higher door than the others. Lamb slid down from the medicine horse and led it easily inside. There were no tracks in the hardpacked earth to betray him. He let the doorskin fall behind him and waited.

He eyed the horse tensely, wondering if it would whicker. But the animal stood calmly and gentle-eyed, as if in some mystic way it knew the sacredness of its life and purposes. Lamb relaxed and drew the skin aside a bit, and peered out.

He had two thoughts: One was to rescue Aspen and Black Wolf. If the soldiers boiled out of the bivouac, leaving only a guard or two, he'd try it. The other, less acceptable, but still worthwhile, was to capture Peter Partridge and hold him hostage. A life for a life. But that would take luck, and just the right circumstances, too.

In the distant dust the captain was bugling his distress like a loon on a lake, and then he and two troopers plunged into the cottonwoods and raced up the creek on Lamb's trajectory, followed half a minute later by a brown blur on a horse—the newspaperman. Lamb felt a keen disappointment. Five or six men were still at the bivouac, and there'd be no way for an old man with a single-shot carbine to spirit her away. It would be even harder to bring along the wounded Black Wolf.

So it had to be the other. Peter was off in the

cottonwoods now, picking his way toward the lodges, trying to catch his brother. The captain and two privates were urging their mounts up the west bank of the creek, and off toward the mountains. Lamb checked his carbine, knowing intuitively that Aspen had loaded it, and then slipped out of the teepee, slithering like a wraith along the dense brush of the creek bank, and finally to a great shaggy tree he knew well. These trees were old friends and summer shade. There he waited, his heart thumping.

Peter trotted close. Lamb sprang out before him, the carbine already sighted upon his chest.

"Raise ye'r hands, boy, or ye'll be dead before ye know."

Peter, startled, considered a split second, and it looked as if he might kick his gelding. Then he turned ashen as he saw the unwavering black bore aimed at his heart, and angrily raised his hands after halting the horse.

"Get ye down, boy, and if ye reach for the revolver, it'll be the last thing ye ever do."

"Damn you, I should have killed you before," Peter said. "You won't get away with this."

"Easy, boy, I have a trembling hand on the trigger these days. Now turn around, back to me, hands on the saddle."

Blanching, Peter turned to face his horse. Lamb flicked the sixgun from Peter's holster and backed swiftly.

"All right, boy, easy now, unbuckle the cartridge belt, eh?"

Peter did.

"Now, lad, take a rein there and walk the pony off to that lodge there, eh? And stay over on this side where we're screened. I'm behind ye, and I've got a twitching finger, I'll tell ye."

They walked carefully to the tallest lodge, Peter muttering under his breath.

"Leave the horse there, and into the lodge with ye."

Peter entered, feeling the bore of his own six-gun in his back.

"Needed to get some thong from my kit to tie ye," Lamb said. "Hands behind ye, now."

Lamb whipped the thong around Peter's crossed wrists swiftly, and knotted it. Then he hung the carbine by its saddle ring thong over the horn, and led his horse.

"Out with ye, now. Ye'll be mounting ye'r horse with ye'r hands tied and I'll help ye up. Just remember, this sixgun is sweating in my old hand, eh?"

It was awkward, but in a moment Peter was up and Lamb was up also, leading the sorrel gelding behind his own horse. The cartridge belt and holster hung over his horn and he dropped the revolver into it.

"Quiet as an Indian now, or ye'll not live to write another lie," said Lamb.

He crossed the creek once again and climbed toward the crest of the hill overlooking the Elk Creek valley, following a shallow coulee up. There was a little dust off to the southwest. It was the private named Fiske who had his rifle at the ready up there, but who plainly didn't know what to do. Lamb rode straight toward him.

"Well, Private, ye can see I'm escaping," Lamb said. "And ye can see I've got the captain's little brother here, and I'll shoot the captain's brother in a trice if ye start lifting that rifle of yours. The captain wouldn't forgive ye for that, would he?"

The private gulped. "No, Sir."

"Well, I came this way to leave a message with the captain, eh, and ye'll deliver it when ye can."

"Yes, Sir."

"I came up here so ye can see I've got this newspaperman here a prisoner. Ye'll tell the captain ye saw me and this boy, eh? And this too. If he does what he's thinking of doing to my wife and my brother-in-law, I'll do what he's thinking of doing to this brother of his here. Follow me, eh?"

"I do, Sir. I'll tell him."

"Good. Now hand me that Springfield and I'll take it a hundred yards or two, and leave it for ye, just in case ye have notions."

"You wouldn't! You wouldn't dare, Lamb!" said Peter, wildly.

Lamb grinned. "The captain said to me, it'd be

all my fault if Aspen were shot because I'd failed to obey his orders. So, boy, I'll say the same to ye. It'd be all his fault if I were forced to shoot ye. Fair enough?"

"You wouldn't. You wouldn't shoot a white man for two dirty Indians," Peter cried.

"On the contrary, lad. I'd shoot a liar of any color for two faithful, loving folks, eh?"

Peter glared whitely. Lamb led the horses north, dropped the sentry's rifle, and then jogged toward the Musselshell valley.

# CHAPTER 10

At dusk, Captain Partridge returned to the bivouac brimming with anger. He and his two soldiers had found nothing. Lamb had given them the slip. The old man knew every crease of these rugged hills and had used that knowledge.

He ordered his men to care for his mount as well as their own and stalked to his shelter. There'd be hell to pay in the morning, he thought savagely. That stupid old man had just condemned his squaw to death, and that buck for good measure.

Corporal Rudeen was waiting for him there, looking as uneasy as a preacher marrying a scarlet woman.

"Begging your pardon, Sir," he began, "I, uh,

relieved the guards, Sir, and went ahead with evening mess. Private Fiske, Sir, uh, had something to report."

"Well?"

"It's about your brother, Sir."

"Well, what of it?"

"He's been taken hostage by Lamb, Sir."

Partridge was thunderstruck. Wildly he peered around the camp, stared into the shelter tent he shared with Peter, turned livid, then red, then deep crimson.

"What happened?"

"We don't know, Sir. Lamb took him, somehow, and bold as you please rode right up that hill there where Fiske was doing sentry duty."

"Why didn't Fiske shoot the bastard?"

"Because, Sir, Lamb had your brother's revolver on him, and also, he says, your brother was ahead, Sir, sort of screening Lamb. Fiske didn't want to risk hitting your brother. And also, since it was your brother coming, he wasn't sure anything was wrong. He didn't know that—"

"That idiot! He should have shot Lamb on the spot. I'll have his neck for this! Where is he?"

In short order, the frightened private was brought to the captain and ordered to report.

"What did Lamb say?" snarled the captain.

"That he'd shoot your brother if you, ah, disposed of your prisoners, Sir."

"Is that all?"

"Yes, Sir. He wanted you to know that. I mean he'd shoot your brother, Sir, if—"

"Idiot! You should have shot Lamb when they left."

"He took my rifle away, Sir."

"Why did you surrender it?"

"Because the sixgun was, ah, pointing at me, and the old man's hands, ah, trembled, Sir. I thought my life was over."

"It probably will be when I'm done with you. You're on report," Partridge roared. "Which way did they go?"

"North, Sir."

"You failed to do your duty, soldier. You're a coward. Did you report this immediately?"

"Yes . . . yes, Sir," Fiske gulped. "Yes. I got my rifle and then ran here."

"Corporal, what did you do when Fiske reported this?"

Rudeen looked uneasy. "I took a man, Ernst, and saddled, and searched for an hour, Sir. We lost the trail in a wooded area with pine needles, but we thought he headed north toward the Musselshell. Then I returned and rotated guards and doubled the guard on the horses, just in case Lamb—"

"Stupid, all of it. You should have ordered every man to mount and go after that renegade. Didn't it occur to you that my brother was being taken captive?"

The corporal was silent.

"Idiots! This army's full of idiots!"

The captain stared at his men, then paced furiously while his troopers peered furtively at him.

"Corporal! I'm going to show Lamb what the United States Army is made of! He thought he got away with something, balanced the odds, saved his squaw, but he didn't. This army keeps its threats, you hear? Keeps its threats. At dawn, if Lamb and those Piegans aren't back here, we execute that squaw and that man. You hear?"

"Yes. . ."

"And then we go after Lamb. We'll catch him somewhere and pull my brother out of it before that renegade learns that his little hostage game failed and the squaw's dead. You understand?"

"Yes, Sir."

"One more thing. Pick a three-man firing squad. Two squads. One for the squaw, and one for the man."

"Sir, uh, begging your pardon, but may I be excused from that?"

"Excused? *Excused?* Of course not. This is the army, not a sewing circle."

"The men, Sir, they won't—"

"They will because I'll order them to." He paused. "I tell you what. Draw lots. Then none of these sissies can complain."

Corporal Rudeen looked disconsolate. "I will do that, Sir." He turned to leave.

"Corporal, I haven't dismissed you," the captain barked. "I'm demoting you. You're a buck private. This whole episode was gross blundering on your part. If my brother dies because of your stupidity I'll come after you, Private Rudeen, and you'll wish you were dead too."

Rudeen's gaze slid to the ground.

"Get out of my sight," the captain barked.

Captain Partridge helped himself to a generous bowl of beans and sowbelly and ate furiously. His whole instinct was to shoot that squaw this instant and saddle up and go after that renegade and Peter right now. But that would be hasty. The army frowned on haste. He would do this in a way that would win the admiration of his commanding officer, Colonel Ambrose. He finished his beans, left the tin plate for the mess detail, and headed for the shelter half, where he intended to begin a written record of events here. It was dusk now, so he lit a field lantern and rummaged around for his pencil.

There was a melancholy upon the camp this evening. Knots of soldiers gathered, whispered, muttered, sank into brooding silence. The trading post was a grim black bulk across the dark meadow. There were no lamps burning within. A deep blue light still glowed behind the western mountains, silhouetting the sawtooth peaks. The night breeze picked up the sweet scent of sage and the sour scent of fear and urine, and wafted it past the captain, past the moths drawn to his field lantern.

Then there was the gloomy bulk of a man outside his tent, standing awkwardly. The captain peered out.

"Yes, Private? Rudeen is it?"

"Yes, Sir. It is . . . ah . . . I have a petition. The men, Sir, asked me—"

"I know what your petition is, Private. The answer is *no,* is that clear?"

"It's cold blood, Sir. She hasn't—what has she done? To die? What has she done, Sir, that we should—"

"Private! That's none of your business. Your business is to accept orders without question. Without *question.* This is the army. Enlisted men do not question their superiors."

There was a long silence. The private's hands squirmed around the brim of his hat.

"This ain't war, Sir. This is just killing for no crime except being Lamb's wife."

"She's a squaw. A savage. She'd torture and mutilate you if this were the other way around."

The private stared at his boots. "Sir . . . every one of us would favor being court-martialed . . . the stockade, Sir, if it come to that. . . ."

"What are you telling me, Rudeen?"

"We don't want to shoot that squaw, Sir. Put us in irons. Put us on report. We don't care. We talked it over and we . . ."

The private's voice faded along with his courage.

"Private," said Partridge icily, "First, you're under arrest. Second, what you have proposed is mutiny. Mutiny, do you understand? Do you know the regulations?"

"Yes."

"Who's involved in this mutiny?"

"All of us."

"And you think you'd get off light, do you? A year in the stockade and then out? A slap on the wrist? Private, do you know what an officer has the right to do in a mutiny?"

He waited. The private was silent.

"Shoot the mutineers, Rudeen. Shoot them dead."

The private twisted his cap in his hands.

"Go tell your conspirators that you'll all be shot, personally, by me, if you mutiny. That you're all on report. That I'm willing to forget this . . . this banal sentimentality about a filthy savage squaw if my orders are obeyed smartly and without question at dawn. And that those who do their duty will get commendations from me. That's all, Private."

The bivouac settled into a somber night, and the soldiers were too far from the trading post to hear the woman in the small slit window weeping.

All day the knowledge had grown in her that her time had come. She had yearned for the sight of her man just once more, and when he did come late in the day on his medicine horse, cleansed and tall in his saddle, with light splintering off of him, alone and unarmed and unafraid in the midst of these army devils—she had rejoiced. Father Sun had given her that last moment, and then that last fleeting goodbye.

She had been ready. She had dragged away the great bed, heavy with soft buffalo robes, and pulled up the boards, and had lifted from the cache a good carbine and a handful of brass shells. These she had slipped into a soft doeskin pouch with a drawstring.

At the same time she had summoned Black Wolf, who had gained strength through the night, and had shown him the cache. He peered into its murk, saw rifles and muskets and ammunition shining dully there. Then, silently, they had lowered the boards, swept dust back into the cracks, and dragged the heavy bed over the cache again. Only then did she speak.

"He is here," she whispered, "and has Father Sun upon him. I have seen it. Soon he will come and I will give him this. He is unarmed now."

He nodded, staring bleakly at her.

"Soon they come to kill me. Maybe you too," she said. "I know. I feel it inside like a medicine woman knows. Maybe I am a medicine woman, Black Wolf."

"It is a good day to die," he grated. "I will sing my songs soon."

"Not today. Tomorrow."

"We could bar the doors and make this trading post a fort. We could use those rifles through the loopholes and kill many bluecoats before we die."

She had been thinking of that. They were in a fortress. The guns in that cache were muzzle-loaders, but she could load while he shot. But there would be four sides to defend, and only one man to shoot, and the bluecoats would rush in.

"You fight if you want," she said. "I will not. If I fight, Richard Lamb will never get his trading post back. My daughters and grandchildren and my sons-in-law would never live here again or have this business to bring them comfort. No. I won't fight. But maybe you fight."

She saw agreement in his eyes.

"If they come, I'll step out first. Then you bar the doors with the heavy poles. You will have time to do what you want, load the guns. . . ."

"I will fight," he said at last. "I will die, and I will take many bluecoats with me."

He smiled wanly and closed his eyes again. "I thought they were friends," he added. "No white man is ever a friend. Not even your man."

She stared at him darkly. She did not want his shadow to go to the Sandhills thinking that. She kneeled beside him and took a cold hand into hers.

"Richard Lamb loves you like a brother," she said softly.

"They are all devils sent to steal our land and our lives. Your man Lamb was one. I would kill them all."

He turned his back to her. She rose, heavy in her heart, and went back to her stool beside the slit window to watch the bluecoats.

She did not want to die. She was too young. She wanted to become an old grandmother, very old, and then, wrapped in a fine robe and placed on a high scaffold, be given to the sun rather than to the cold earth, high in a cottonwood beside this creek. Then her shadow would be pleased before it flew to the Sandhills.

She ached to see Tall Grass Bending just once again. Tall Grass, her girl with the two bloods to make her beautiful. Lamb had named her Hope, the white man name, and said Hope meant good wanting. That was a good name. And her thoughts turned to her other girl, Spring Willow, delicate like the willow leaves after the Cold Maker left. Faith, she was called in the other tongue, trusting-in-the-good he had explained, and she liked that too. They were a long way away now, and so were her fine brown grandchildren, proud Siksika children for a future time.

Richard Lamb had come and gone and she knew that he had taken Peter with him, but it would not be enough to save her. He had ridden to the window and whispered love and had taken her offering and had galloped away while Father

145

Sun shielded him. She revered that moment, when she saw him through the slit window and saw strong medicine even in one so old. It was good.

She smelled the sage and the night air and saw the blue of last light behind the western mountains, and she ached for life, for the world she was leaving, for the simple sight of waving grass and stars and laughing creeks and sun upon brown cheeks. She thought of washing her blue black hair until it squeaked in the water. She wanted to be free, to feel the good earth beneath her moccasins, and to walk through aspens and see the leaves shake in the sunlight the way her spirit did.

There was shouting out there and she saw the captain and heard enough to know how things stood. Then there was silence and knots of bluecoats whispering, and one young one going to the captain in the dark, and then more shouts and threats, and the captain saying he would shoot the bluecoats if they didn't obey. She understood.

She was saddened for the heart of Black Wolf, who could no longer see what she saw, that there were white men like the captain and his short-pants brother, and other white men like her husband and the bluecoats who did not want to kill her; that there were all kinds of white men, good and bad, just as there were all kinds of Siksika, good and bad, some with great medicine who cared for the poor and the widows, and some who beat their women and had darkness in their eyes. But Black Wolf had turned his back on her, and on that knowledge, and he would kill all he could before they killed him.

She cried. Tomorrow she would not let them see her tears and her face would be a hard mask. But now she cried, for the life was going away and she would not breathe sweet air, or shiver when the Cold Maker came, or hold Richard Lamb in her warm arms beneath the buffalo robes.

She wept softly through the lonely hours, watching the bluecoats sleep through the night. She wept for the sun and for the moon, and she said to the Great One that her man had called God, "Why?"

They fetched her at dawn, Captain Partridge and two soldiers whose faces were pasty white beneath their tans. When she opened the massive plank door they were surprised. She looked beautiful, with a beauty they had never seen or imagined possible in an Indian woman. She wore a ceremonial dress of the softest cream doeskin, fringed at the hem and delicately beaded across the bodice with the symbols of the sun and clouds and lightning. A crimson sash of silk was knotted at her waist. On her feet were fine, beaded black moccasins of soft elkskin, and around her neck was a large necklace of polished grizzly bear claws, with long black beads in between. She had plaited her hair into two lustrous braids, which hung down over her breast, and at the end of each was a bow of red ribbon. In her hand was Richard Lamb's sacred book, with black leather covers, the one he called the Bible.

They did not tell her why they had come, but there were tears flowing from the corners of her black marble eyes, tears she could not contain, and they knew that she knew. The captain's revolver was drawn, but pointed at the two soldiers rather than at her.

"I am ready now," she said, but she wasn't, and her voice broke. "I am not a good Siksika woman," she added. Carefully she closed the great door behind her and there was a second thud, as if the bolt had fallen after she closed it.

"Why do you do this?" she asked. "Why me?"

"Do what?" the captain replied. "We are just going for a walk."

She stared at him from a tear-streaked face, and he turned his head away and whistled tunelessly.

"Why do you do this?" she asked the bluecoat at her left.

He was silent for a moment, and then, harshly: "To stay alive."

He nodded toward the revolver pointed at his belly.

"Woman, silence!" snapped Partridge.

"Why?" she said. "Why do you do this?"

The captain reddened. "I told you to be quiet."

"Quiet? Soon I'll be quiet. Maybe you are a savage. Siksika warriors don't kill women and children. Sometimes. Almost never. But white soldiers kill women and children."

"I don't know what you're talking about. Be silent or I will take measures."

They were walking toward the creek, toward the cottonwoods, toward a majestic cottonwood whose green branches spread lovingly over the meadow. It was the queen of the cottonwoods.

"Why do you do this?" she asked the other soldier, Ernst, who pressed his lips thin and refused to answer.

"Quiet!"

The other bluecoats huddled close to their cookfire, not seeing, not wanting to see.

"You tell me why you're doing this, and maybe I'll be quiet." Her feet were refusing to step ahead.

"I don't know what you're talking about," said the captain with a cracked voice. "It's a nice morning."

"You got no truth," she replied. "You are not a gentleman who gives word. You give me word of honor you will not shoot me?"

"Yes, of course, just a walk," said the captain.

"Some honor, gentleman," said Aspen. "Why do you do this?"

Some berserk force exploded in the captain and he lashed at her with the butt of his revolver. It glanced off her head, stunning her, and she fell.

On the ground, her eyes unfocused, she stared up at him. "Why do you do this?" she asked.

He exploded again, wildly, booting her in the ribs. She huddled in a heap, clutching her chest.

"Lift her up," he yelled at the soldiers. They stared at him, paralyzed. "Lift her up and drag her there or I'll kill you."

They did. They dragged her to the shaggy gray trunk of the cottonwood and propped her there. She was beautiful.

"Why do you do this?" she muttered to him.

Shaking, he waved the soldiers away, waved them toward the third soldier, Private Pinski, twenty yards distant, his revolver weaving wildly at them every step. They formed a line.

"Present arms," he said.

"I'll tell you why you do this," she said. "You do this because—"

"Ready!" he screamed.

"Aim! Fire!"

Three ragged shots cracked from the Springfields.

She stood, staring at them, untouched. The smell of burnt powder drifted across the dawn.

"You do this because you're not a man like your father, and not a man like Richard Lamb."

Her voice was strong in its pain, and sang clearly through the cool air to the soldiers huddling at the fire. She drew herself up, head high.

"You're a liar," she said. "The son of the devil."

Captain Partridge stared at her, stared at the three soldiers. "You'll rot in a stockade the rest of your lives," he said.

He stormed toward Aspen, revolver in hand, and at a distance of three feet fired into her face. She slumped to the earth, dead, a blue hole in her forehead. He glared at her in the stretching silence.

"Pinski. Drag her out of here. Ernst, Fiske, go get that buck." The revolver was leveled at them.

Reluctantly they trudged toward the trading post. Ernst swung his Springfield around toward the captain, remembered it wasn't loaded, and stumbled wearily. It seemed a long walk from the cottonwood to the post.

From the slit window of the post there was the low boom of a flintlock, and Private Moriarty Fiske fell dead with a lead ball through his heart. A moment later there was the crack of a caplock and Private Armand Ernst fell mortally wounded with a ball through his right lung. It had been less than two years since he had arrived in the New World with hope in his heart.

It took a few moments for anyone to react, and by then Private Olaf Rudeen, at the cookfire, had been knocked senseless by a ball that grazed his temple, and Private Artemus Goldsmith had taken a ball through his left forearm.

Another ball, this one from a battered old

Pennsylvania longrifle that still shot accurately, blew the campaign cap off the head of Captain Partridge and riffled his hair. The shot galvanized him.

"Around the back," he bellowed, emptying his sixgun at the slit window. Private Johnny Johnson came running. A crack from the window hit his Springfield and bloodied Johnson's hand, and he dropped the rifle and dove toward the captain. They were both safe, close to the rear door of the post. The captain tried the door and found it barred.

"So!" said the captain, "there were some arms in there after all."

He peered around the corner of the building and saw a barrel protruding from the slit window. The men at the cookfire had taken cover in the cottonwoods, dragging their wounded with them.

From within the post there were random shots now, from one slit window and then another. A horse dropped, shot through the neck. The captain knew he didn't have men enough left to storm the place, not even against one wounded man with some loaded flintlocks.

"We'll have to burn the bastard out."

There was dry grass at hand, and twigs and debris near the base of the verandah. Swiftly he gathered grass and tinder in a mound against the log wall under the verandah, and poured powder from three cartridges over it, after biting out the bullets. Then he touched a flaming lucifer to it. The powder sizzled and flared, catching the grass and kindling. In a few minutes the south wall of the post was aflame, along with the whole verandah. In another ten minutes, that side of the building was an inferno and the captain and the private were able to creep away to the security of the far meadows.

There came from within the high harsh sound of a man chanting, the plaintive death song of a warrior en route to the Sandhills. Within an hour the trading post was engulfed, and orange flame jagged into the sky beneath a pillar of black smoke that could be seen for a hundred miles. The chanting had ceased.

Back at the bivouac, the wounded had been cared for. The uninjured were hastily burying the dead. The remaining horses were being saddled and packed. There were two dead and three wounded. The captain decided the wounded could all travel, but they would be useless. Since Murphy had not returned from Fort Ellis, that left Partridge with four men in fighting condition, and maybe Rudeen, when he recovered.

But the captain was not done. While the men climbed their mounts, he stalked to the cotton-woods and found Aspen lying in the brush. With his saber, he hacked off her head and grabbed it by one of the braids. He carried it to the livestock pen where he jammed it down upon a post. He knew Indians. He knew that once they saw it, they'd never return here again.

He returned and mounted.

"Now we'll get Lamb, too," he said dispassionately. "And rescue my brother. It'll be easy."

The seven men under his command stared blankly at him, and said nothing.

# CHAPTER 11

They would come after him. Richard Lamb was sure they would try to rescue Peter. He didn't know when or how, or how much time he had.

He could no longer see distant things and that bothered him. The weakness of his old body, his one eye, could betray him. If he headed across the open plains, they would see him before he saw them. And even if he discerned movement, he'd have trouble determining how many troopers there were and how fast they were travelling.

The plains would not do. He chose the mountains. Now they were crossing the wide open grasslands north of the Musselshell River, leaving tracks that any pilgrim could follow. But in the mountains he'd have a better chance. In the mountains he'd give the pursuers the slip, as he had many times during his years as a trapper.

Peter Partridge rode sullenly, the heat of anger radiating out from him. The old man watched him closely. The newsman was obviously looking for ways to escape, his mind and senses awhirl with possibilities. Lamb knew the attempt would be made sooner or later. He hoped sooner. It would settle something.

Ahead of them rose the dark forested bulk of the Little Belt Mountains, the slopes gentle and uninspiring compared to the lofty crags of the Crazies. They rode their horses northward in a shallow draw where they would not be skylined. In the spring it probably ran water into the Musselshell but it was dry now, with lush grasses in the bottoms.

"Ye're thinking of escaping," he said to Peter. "It's written all over ye. Ye're thinking I'm an old man, and I'll be needing sleep, and sooner or later ye'll snatch the sixgun or the carbine, and then ye'll march me back to ye'r brother—if he doesn't catch us first, eh?"

Peter looked startled, and then nodded.

"But he'll not catch us. He's got no scouts, no trackers worth anything. Army's helpless out here without them. Not a lot of men have those skills, and none in ye'r party, I imagine."

"Where are we going?" Peter asked.

"I'm debating it," Lamb replied. "Fort Shaw, most likely."

Peter gaped, wild hope in his eyes.

"But not until Aspen's freed and on the reservation."

"And where will we go in the meantime?"

"Nowhere. Dodge the army. It might take months, but that's easy to do in this country."

"With me a prisoner? Sooner or later I'll—"

"Ye'll try, but ye won't succeed."

"Sooner or later—"

"I have friends, ye understand."

"You'll hang for this, Lamb!"

"Ye've already said I'd hang for assorted other crimes." Lamb smiled amiably.

"Take me to Fort Shaw, and I'll put in a good word—"

"Politics, eh?" He grunted. "A good word. Those who live by politics die by politics. There are times when ye should beat ye'r politics into swords. Shall I take ye at ye'r word? How good is ye'r word?"

Peter reddened.

The coulee curled upward and soon they were riding past lone ponderosas, outposts of the forested slopes ahead. Lamb paused in the shadow of one tree on a rise, and peered backward. He saw nothing and wasn't sure he could see anything even if something were there. But it was not a weakness that Peter knew about.

"Well?" Lamb asked gently.

"This doesn't mean anything," Peter replied. "Joe will come."

Lamb smiled.

"How do you expect to feed us?" Peter asked crossly. His stomach rumbled.

"The way men of the wilderness have always fed themselves. Except when there's poor doings."

Peter did not know the particulars of wilderness survival, and Lamb didn't choose to enlighten him.

For two hours more they climbed a wooded cleft in the mountains, following a rocky watershed where a few pools still remained. At one such pool, from which a side canyon branched, Lamb called a halt.

"We'll rest the horses," he said. "I'll untie ye."

"High time. I'm hungry."

The old man stiffly eased off the great medicine horse, limped over to his prisoner, and freed him.

"Ye wouldn't be thinking of using those free hands on me, would ye, lad?"

Peter glowered and dismounted, while Lamb led the horses to lush grass and tied their hackamores to a picket of thong. The weary animals snorted and gorged on the tender June grasses.

"When are you going to feed me?" It was a demand, not a question.

"I heard ye before, lad. When I'm ready to. If feeding ye takes a half hour, the captain can gain maybe two miles, eh?"

"What are you going to shelter us with? I've

nothing but the clothes on my back and these nights are cold."

Lamb grinned. "Ye didn't think of that last night when ye left me without a robe, did ye?"

"You're used to the hard life here. I'm not."

"Ye'll be getting used to it fast now."

Peter's horse snorted, raised its head, and stopped chewing grass. A moment later it dropped a pile of steaming green horseapples. It was something the old man had been waiting for.

"Get up, lad. Put those apples in ye'r bandana and drop them over in that side canyon, about twenty yards up."

"What?"

"Ye heard me. Do it, or it'll go hard for ye."

Reluctantly Peter did as he was bid under the watchful eye of the old man. Then he washed his hands and the bandana.

"It wouldn't fool a scout for more than a minute," Lamb said. "But it might fool the army."

Peter glared.

"Now we'll walk. Lead ye'r horse, lad, and let it rest. We'll walk a while and then ride till dark. Maybe beyond dark."

"That's ten at night! And I haven't eaten!"

"Ye have it right."

They walked up the canyon for a half hour, the old man behind the sullen newspaperman. Then they mounted again and rode through the thickening twilight. The New Yorker was raging.

In the rocky streambed they were leaving very few tracks.

Lamb, weary himself from the long day, halted them at a high rocky place strewn with gray slab-rock. It was dusk.

"Are we stopping here?"

"No, lad, we're going over that saddle and into the next drainage." He pointed west, perpendicular to their trail. "Turn now, and stay on that rock."

Peter glared but did as he was told. The horses clattered their way up the flank of the valley, where a sea of blue twilight greeted them at the top of the ridge. They had left little sign. Even a good tracker would be thrown off—for a while.

On the ridge they scared up a muley doe. She stared and then leisurely trotted off. Richard Lamb did nothing.

"Why didn't you shoot her?" the newsman snapped.

"I like her alive. And shots carry far from the ridges."

He did not tell the newsman that the doe was a few days from fawning.

They plunged downslope through thick forest, and at the bottom it was black. Lamb stopped in a small park where the grass was high. There was only the light of the stars and a faint northern afterglow across the arctic heavens.

"We'll stop here," he said, easing lamely to the

ground. Peter followed. "Dry camp and no fire," Lamb added.

"And no food."

Lamb did not reply. There was pemmican in his kit but he did not intend to share it, not just now. The humbling had to come first.

"Sit down there while I tend the horses," Lamb directed. He unsaddled both animals and tied them to the picket. Quietly, in the dark, he lifted his carbine from the saddle sheath, pulled the .44 cartridge from it, and slipped it into his pocket along with the others Aspen had given him. Then he slid the carbine back into its sheath and carried the saddle back to the camp.

"That was only a horsehair pad under ye'r McClellan," he said, "but ye'll get some warmth from it, and ye'r saddle will make ye a pillow."

Under his own saddle was a folded blanket that would suffice, as it had many times in the past, as a bedroll.

"Hands behind ye'r back. I've got to truss ye up for the night, now."

Peter didn't move.

"Do it, lad, or it'll not go easy for ye."

"How can I sleep with my hands tied behind me?" Peter snarled.

"Same way as I slept with heavy manacles on mine," Lamb replied. "Do it! It may be dark, but not so dark ye don't see the sixgun pointing at ye."

Peter Partridge glared at the black weapon in

the old man's wavering hand. "What if I give you my word of honor that—that I won't try anything?"

"Word? Why should I trust ye? Ambitious young fellow ready to do anything, anything at all, to get ahead? Honor? What's that to ye? It's not even in ye'r head."

"You have my word," Peter said sullenly.

Lamb paused to consider. Or, rather, paused long enough to give that impression. "Well," he said reluctantly, "I have ye'r word, do I?"

"Yes."

"Ye'll stay put, and not try to break away?"

"Yes. I promise."

"I'll trust ye, then. I'm right tired, and I'll roll in."

Lamb could almost feel Peter's scornful exuberance cutting through the night air. Carefully he scraped away the pebbles under his bed and laid grasses beneath his blanket. Quietly he drew the medicine horse to him until it stood above him like a great gray ghost in the night. Then he wrapped himself in the blanket and drew the sixgun from its holster. He would sleep. He figured Peter would wait until dawn to try anything because he wouldn't want to sit up all night holding that carbine on the old man. Richard Lamb was exhausted. His stomach growled its hunger, although he had noticed in old age that hunger wasn't as much with him as it had been when he was young. His old bones ached. But the saddle blanket, pungent with horse sweat, was warm, and he slipped into an easy sleep almost instantly.

He awoke, rested, at false dawn, his senses alerting him to subtle change, as they had during all his dangerous years as a lone young trapper in this wild. In the murky gray light he made out the dark bulk of Peter looming over the saddle, silently slipping the carbine from its sheath.

Within the blanket, Lamb lifted the sixgun and aimed it. The medicine horse, still standing faithfully above the old man, lifted its head sharply. Peter Partridge had the carbine out now, a finger on the trigger, the butt plate in his shoulder. And he was stalking forward, toward Lamb, toward point-blank range.

"Lamb!" he roared, the voice shattering the peace. "I've got you now. Hands up. Get out of that roll."

Lamb eyed him lazily and tossed the blanket aside. In his hand was the revolver.

"Some word ye give," he said drily. "Some honor ye have."

"Drop it. Or I'll shoot."

"Give it a try if ye wish. It's not loaded."

Peter stared, thunderstruck. Then, obviously assuming the old man was lying, he grinned and aimed at the old man's heart. He pulled the trigger. It snapped quietly. He stared.

"Some word ye give, lad. And ye call ye'rself civilized. Honorable. I'll tell ye something. It's

pemmican, but he didn't. Instead, he steered toward a gray rimrock where, some instinct told him, there might be game.

There was. A wolf stared at them unafraid, on its haunches, curious about creatures he had never seen. It would do, Lamb decided. He rather enjoyed what would come. He signaled the newsman to halt. The man had seen nothing and was observing this wilderness through city eyes. Lamb slid the carbine out, peered down its notched sight until the muzzle aimed at the wolf's breast . . . and squeezed. And missed. Smoothly Lamb ejected the cartridge, homed another, swung toward the trotting wolf, and shot. The sound seemed small and lost in this wild. But the wolf somersaulted and lay still.

"A dog. You've shot a dog."

"A wolf."

Partridge paused. "You expect me to eat a wolf?"

"Lad, in this land ye eat whatever God gives ye."

Lamb reloaded and studied the country. There had been no one on the back trail. The shot had been muffled by the great forests beyond the plateau. And he doubted that the United States Army was anywhere near. Still he waited. As a young trapper he had saved his life several times by waiting. Then he rode to the wolf.

Peter stared at it with compressed lips. "Dog meat. It makes me sick to think of it."

Lamb said nothing. He slipped off the white horse, tied thong around the wolf's neck, and dragged it to a tree. It was heavy. Shakily he hoisted the carcass and tied it up. Then he gutted it swiftly.

"Build a fire," he said.

"I haven't a lucifer."

Lamb stared, and from his kit extracted a steel striker and flint. He soon had a tiny bundle of cottony tinder flaring. Sullenly, the newsman added sticks.

Lamb peeled back the shaggy pelt with sharp jerks and then sliced warm flank meat from the animal and set it to roasting on green spits he cut from willow brush. Wolf it may have been, but the smell of the sizzling flesh set his mouth to watering.

Peter sat disconsolately, seeing a feast and preferring famine. Lamb let him sit. He cut more meat and started it roasting, and then unsaddled the horses and picketed them in the strong timothy grass. He brushed their backs with handfuls of old grasses, and examined their hoofs.

When the wolf meat was well browned, he pulled it off the spits with his knife and let it cool on a flat rock. He had no utensils; he would eat with his fingers. He sliced more from the carcass, reloaded the willow spits, and set them roasting. Peter's eyes followed every move with sullen contempt.

The old man ate. Wolf meat was almost taste-less, especially without salt or seasoning. And it was a soft, gummy meat. But it filled his belly and he felt his strength return almost miraculously as he sat in the grass. He ate again, and set still more of the wolf to roasting. When he had cut what he could off the flanks, he began on the haunches until he had cut several more pounds of the flesh. Periodically he paused to pull the roasted meat from the fire and set it to cool.

He tended the horses then, or appeared to, examining their legs for heat, scrubbing mud off their coats. He led them to one of the springs and let them drink leisurely, until they nuzzled the water playfully and swallowed no more. When he returned, the pile of roasted wolfmeat was gone. It was what he had hoped.

It was midday. "Time to be off, lad," he said amiably.

He dropped the carcass and recovered his thong.

"Aren't you going to take any with us?"

"Do ye want to eat more wolf?"

"But we might not . . ." The voice faded.

Lamb waited politely for Peter to finish. Then they mounted. Lamb paused a moment, studying their back trail. There was nothing to see, so he touched his heels to the horse.

He had thought at first of Fort Shaw. Some of the officers there knew him; all knew of him. But the more he pondered that, the less he liked it, with the Partridges poisoning that well. He was worried about his daughters and his kin, especially if Captain Partridge should overtake them. The man was capable of anything. They would be travelling north down the Smith River, and he guessed the captain was not far behind by now. He worried, too, about that dispatch rider that Partridge had sent to Fort Ellis—a dispatch that could send a swarm of troopers out, troopers who might shoot first and ask questions later. Of course, his old friend Barney Beeman was there, in command. . . .

He decided to try to find his kin. Abruptly, they veered from north to northwest, angling closer to the canyon of the Smith. The newsman didn't know where he was, and said nothing.

Lamb thought of Aspen, safe back at the post as far as he knew. Surely the captain would not harm her if his own brother's life were at stake. But Lamb felt uneasy about it. Some dark menace hung over her. Was it only a few days ago, when the soldiers came, that she announced that her time had come? She had uncanny instincts, and that pronouncement, heavy in his mind now, clawed at him. He turned and glared at Peter Partridge, and then pushed his medicine horse into a steady jog.

# CHAPTER 12

Fort Ellis had been a great place for his final posting, thought Colonel Barnabas Beeman. He didn't really want to retire. From his glassed window, one of the few on the post, he had a splendid view westward across the sun-drenched Gallatin Valley to the great blue snow-shrouded mountains in every direction. Behind him and flanking off northward were the Bridgers. Off to the west, the Tobacco Roots. Nearer, south and west, the Gallatins and Madisons, both part of the Yellowstone country.

Maybe, he thought, he would stay on as a sutler. Then he laughed at that. They wouldn't know what to do with him once they didn't have to salute, and his replacement would resent his presence. In any case, Fort Shaw was the quartermaster post for the area as well as regimental headquarters.

Still . . . it was hard to let go after a lifetime of boots and saddles, the crack of carbines, the hiss of arrows, and hoarse cries of war. He remembered the proud blue line at dress parade, thought of the yellow chevrons and stripes that said *horse soldier.* And, above all, the men, the comrades under fire, old soldiers fading away. . . .

A day's ride to the west was the Three Forks

country where the Gallatin, Jefferson, and Madison Rivers joined to form the mighty Missouri. Maybe he'd settle there, run some cattle on that fine grass, and sell them to the gold camps. This had all been Blackfeet hunting country once, and the buffalo had been thick here. But their numbers dwindled now. The Blackfeet and buffalo both had been pushed north bit by bit as the Bozeman Trail disgorged its horde of fortune-seekers, heading for Virginia City, Confederate Gulch, Bannock, and Last Chance Gulch. Now all he saw of the Blackfeet was an occasional hunting or horse-stealing band, slipping down from the new Indian Agency up on Badger Creek.

This was a peaceful place, too, a fitting final assignment for an old rogue cavalryman with four months left. Not a post for a man with large ambitions, he mused; not a post for the likes of his acquaintance George Custer, who had run for the presidency across the high plains of the Northern Cheyenne and Sioux. There was trouble out there, but not here, where a day's work consisted of patrolling this stretch of the trail. Last summer, the Sioux and Cheyenne had sent runners, immediately after the Little Bighorn, inviting the Blackfeet federation to join them, but the Blackfeet had declined, and so things were peaceful here in the West. Not that the traffic on the trail was heavy anymore. Ever since Red Cloud had shut down the trail in 1868, the real mission of Fort Ellis had been to provide a buffer between the gold mines and the warring plains Indians.

He heard a clatter out in the parade ground and then his aide, Lieutenant Januarius Coleman, loomed in the doorway.

"Dispatch, sir," he said.

A moment later a dusty, trail-worn infantry private entered and saluted. He had a leather pouch in hand.

"Private Aloysius Murphy, Sor, Company H, Fort Shaw."

It was from the field, then, he thought. It would have been telegraphed otherwise.

"At ease, soldier. You have something for me?"

Murphy handed him the pouch.

"You look tired, Private. Have a seat. I will no doubt have questions."

Beeman pulled out three papers. The dispatch was from Partridge up at Shaw. He knew the man; he knew most of the officers here in the West. A competent man, Partridge, but with Custer's ambition: a man, Beeman thought, who never lived in the present because he was obsessed with his future. Yes, that was it. A man without the present in him. The colonel adjusted his gold-rimmed half-spectacles, which rode low on his ruddy wide nose.

" 'CO, Ellis,' " he read. " 'Request assistance rounding up Blackfeet hostiles, all kin of trader,

Lamb, on Musselshell, probably heading south or west. Request wire report to CO, Fort Shaw. Murphy will supply details.' "

Beeman frowned. Lamb? Those Piegans at Lamb's post . . . hostiles? Old Lamb, rooted there forever and a friend of all, with hostiles? It was incredible.

The other papers, written on foolscap, addressed to the editor of the *New York Herald* . . . he'd get to them in a minute.

"Private Murphy."

The private sprang up.

"Tell me," the colonel said. "Tell me all about this."

"Well, Sor . . . well, Sor . . . ," Murphy faltered.

"Relax, soldier, and start at the beginning. What was this mission?"

"To remove all Blackfeet to the reservation, Sor, because of hostilities."

"Even Lamb's family?"

"Yes, Sor. And they didn't want to go, Sor. At least not right away, like the cap'n ordered."

"Right away?"

"Yes, Sor, the cap'n wanted them to saddle up and go right away and—"

"Saddle right up? Just go?"

"Yes, Sor, leave immediately. Shut down the post and come. He confiscated some old flint-locks and caplocks and some ammunition . . ."

"And Lamb? What'd he do?"

"Protested, Sor, so the cap'n's brother shot him—"

"Shot? Resisted?"

"Yes, Sor, not bad, though, a crease on his cheek. Lamb, he was trying to delay, get his Injun folk some time to pack up their goods and get squared away and all."

It scarcely made sense to Colonel Beeman. Unless Partridge was forcing the issue for some reason.

"Who's the captain's brother—who shot Lamb?"

"A New York newsman, Sor."

"I see. Then what happened?"

Private Murphy stood uneasily, not wanting to talk about the rest. "Well, Sor . . ."

"Yes?" The colonel waited patiently, staring at the flag, the regimental colors, and finally the mountains on the western horizon.

"Well, Sor . . . Lamb and Missus Lamb, they protested maybe too sharp, and those Injuns, they decided they wouldn't go, at least just then, or maybe it was they'd go in the mornin' but not that day, after they got themselves packed and the travois made and the lodges took down."

"And?"

"The cap'n, Sor, he got mad and tortured one. Lamb's brother-in-law, as a matter of fact. Put a blade to his ribs, but that didn't work. They said they'd rather die there than starve up in the reservation. So they started on old Lamb—"

*"Lamb!"*

"Yes, Sor. But Lamb backed him off and told him the young men was up in the hills ready to shoot us."

"How large was your unit?"

"A squad, Sor. The Injuns got the horses out—not our horses, theirs, and that made the cap'n . . . ah . . . unhappy, Sor."

"What about Lamb? Is he badly wounded? Alive?"

"I don't know, Sor. He was under arrest, manacled."

*"Arrest?* For what?"

"I don't know what all, Sor. He broke a horse jaw, I think. Talked back at the cap'n. Cap'n could say better than me, Sor. Anyways, the Injuns pulled out at night and then they sneaked back and got Lamb right out of our bivouac, bold as you please. When morning come around, that's when the cap'n dispatched me, Sor. He's going after the Injuns and going to arrest Lamb again and wants help. Last they knew, the Injuns and Lamb took off into the Crazies, least that's where the tracks, travois tracks—they got their goods with them, but not their lodges—that's where all the tracks went."

It was incredible, grotesque. Beeman stared, uncertain of what to do.

"Do you think the army pushed too hard, Private?"

"Can't say, Sor."

"Of course, I understand."

Barney Beeman rapped his fingers on the pine-plank desk and then turned to the newspaper dispatches from Peter Partridge.

"Cap'n's brother wants those wired, Sor, collect if possible. Asked me to ask you. Cap'n said they could go if they didn't interfere with military traffic."

The colonel adjusted his sliding half-spectacles again and read the dispatches, growing more and more flushed. By the time he was done he was in a rage. But, he reminded himself, there was an enlisted man present.

"Why was Peter Partridge along on this . . . assignment?"

"Wouldn't know, Sor."

"Was he dishing out a lot of advice to the captain?"

"I couldn't say, Sor."

The colonel smiled. "Yes of course . . . Lieutenant, this man has travelled far and fast. I'd like him to be well fed immediately, even if you have to scare up the cooks. And find him private quarters to rest; I'll have more questions later. And of course make sure his mounts are looked after.

"Private Murphy, thank you. You've traveled a long way, and bravely. The lieutenant will see you to your quarters and comforts. By the way, what are your further instructions?"

175

"Return to Lamb's post, Sor, and look for written instructions if no one is there. But he expected Missus Lamb, at least, with her guards, to be there. She's under arrest also, Sor."

"Aspen? What did *she* do?"

"She sassed—ah, I don't know, Sor."

The colonel grinned. "Dismissed," he said. He knew Aspen.

There was a lot more he intended to ask and needed to know. But he was in no hurry and wanted to think through his questions carefully. Impending retirement did that, gave a man some perspective. He stood, and stared across the sea of grass to the brooding mountains. He'd feed the trooper, let him rest, and then find out the rest.

He read the newsman's dispatches once again. Barney Beeman was a brick-colored man in any case, but now he was redder still. Preposterous, he thought. Lamb a renegade, Lamb a gun-runner to the hostiles. Didn't that New Yorker know that Lamb's post was a hundred miles or more too far west? And that Lamb sold to the Blackfeet, the Crow, the Shoshone, and the Flathead sometimes? Only some idiot easterner would jump to such wild—but no, maybe it wasn't idiocy. Maybe it was calculation. Lies, to be blunt about it. The work of a mendacious climber who knew exactly how to stir the pot and profit from it. Make scapegoats—God knows, the whole country was looking for a scapegoat to blame for the Little

Bighorn—and . . . make heroes. Two heroes, to be precise. A glory-hungry newsman, and an ambitious captain, who perhaps wanted to become major, colonel, general, senator, governor, president.

Where was it, the colonel wondered, that he had first met Partridge? During the war, somewhere. A rich young man, a bought or finagled lieutenancy . . . and surprising competence of a sort after that. The sort that avoided mistakes and did things by book and rote and drill. At least until now.

And why now? Probably that brother. Those dispatches were either the work of a total greenhorn . . . or a liar. And he bet on the latter. If he sent those dispatches the whole country would be in an uproar. And old Lamb would be the sacrifice. The *Sacrificial Lamb.* But not on the altar of God. On the altar of Partridge ambition.

Gun-runner indeed. The worst old Lamb was guilty of was selling a little illegal whiskey to the Indians. It was how the traders survived. Maybe he didn't even do that: Lamb had a brisk trade with the mining camps. Those Blackfeet kin of his were forever herding cattle through the Gallatin valley, here, en route to the camps, or driving wagonloads of produce or even native hay. Why, he knew most of those Blackfeet by sight. Hostiles? Not unless Partridge deliberately forced them to turn hostile, if even then.

That Partridge, hollow man if ever there was

one, Beeman mused. He always knew there was something not quite right about the captain. Couldn't sit down over bourbon and branch with the man and feel at home . . . or even feel present with him.

Barney Beeman was suddenly tired. He'd come here to HQ after the evening mess, not because there was anything to do here, but because he couldn't stand being alone in his quarters. He had never married and now it seemed too late; he was getting on. And his spartan bachelor quarters howled his loneliness back at him each evening, forcing him to pour too much bourbon. So he was here, in the twilight, puttering in his office. And, wherever he was, there was his faithful adjutant —and shadow—Januarius Coleman.

What to do? There were things to consider. Things that protocol required, such as wiring Glenn Ambrose at Fort Shaw. But there were things he was free *not* to do, and one of them, by God, was sending those newspaper dispatches. He'd hold them. And he would justify holding them if he had to. Not that he gave a damn now, with his retirement on the horizon.

He lit a kerosene lamp in the gloomy room, and the light made him think more clearly.

There was Lamb to consider, and his Aspen. Both under military detention! He doubted that the old trader was guilty of anything, and neither were his Blackfeet kin. They were all from the

Small Robes Band, Lamb had once told him, the southernmost of the Piegan bands. And now, except for those skin lodges, they were living a settled life not much different from that of the whites who were pouring in. The army should hold them up as a model instead of chasing them back to their reservations. Yes, there was that order, it had come to all the forts. But officers all had some discretion, some leeway, in interpreting these things.

Barney Beeman sat down in his straight-backed desk chair and began to compose a dispatch to Ambrose. It had to be done. But the wording would be important. The right wording might save a lot of bloodshed and grief.

"Lieutenant," he called.

Coleman appeared at the door.

"Send this to Fort Shaw."

On the foolscap Beeman had written, *Partridge requests reinforcements to locate and escort trader Lamb Piegans.*

That was all. No mention of hostiles. Yet, in its narrow way, it was exactly what Captain Partridge had asked him to do. But, Beeman thought, it now put the onus on the captain. Ambrose would scarcely call out his troops, and would probably do nothing at all.

"One more thing," Beeman added, handing Coleman the sheet. "I'm taking a platoon myself to Lamb's Post immediately after morning mess.

Draw it from Company C tonight. I'll want field rations for a week, spare mounts, and a farrier sergeant with us. Have fresh mounts for Private Murphy, I'm taking him with us. And notify Captain Wright that he'll be acting CO. Let Murphy rest, tell him in the morning."

"I'll have everything ready, Sir," said Januarius.

Barney Beeman frowned. He didn't like to leave the post in the hands of anyone so junior. He could be faulted for that, especially if trouble arose. But what the hell. He'd be out of this man's army soon. . . .

Dammit, he thought, I want a scout, too. A tracker. Maybe that half-Crow if he's around and sober. No, not a Crow. That'd be an act of war against those people.

He scribbled a message to Coleman, asking for a Blackfeet-speaking scout, and left it on Coleman's desk.

The small blue column was off at six, ranked in twos. Beeman led them out to the trail, and then east over the Bozeman Pass. At the summit he called a halt to let men and animals rest. He intended to travel with all deliberate speed, but not in urgent haste. When the column had formed again, he asked his sergeant to send Private Murphy to him. The infantry dispatch rider approached timidly, and reined in beside the colonel.

"Sor?"

"A fine day to be travelling, is it not, Private Murphy?"

"A fine day indeed, Sor."

"Ever thought of transferring to the cavalry, lad? Would those yella chevrons please you more than the white?"

"I'm proud of the Infantry, Sor."

"A good attitude, Private. But if you wish to become a cavalry trooper here at Fort Ellis, I'll transfer you here and now. It's easy, you know. All I have to do is send them a replacement at Fort Shaw."

"Well, Sor, it's mighty tempting."

"Say the word and it's done, Private Murphy. No need even to return to Fort Shaw. We'll do the paperwork and have your gear freighted down here. You ride well, a hundred miles in a day and a half, and the horses in decent shape, too. I just thought I'd ask."

Murphy thought a moment, while the colonel waited patiently.

"Sor, I'll do it. If there's no complications with, uh, Cap'n Partridge."

The colonel beamed. "Consider it done, Trooper Murphy. Now, then, tell me about this whole business. Don't spare me any details. Start at Fort Shaw and tell me all that happened up until the moment you were dispatched here. Better yet, start with the newsman, the civilian."

"He's the cap'n's brother, Sor, and I'm just an enlisted man. I don't want to get myself into trouble in this army. . . ."

"Yes, of course, Trooper. I understand perfectly. I don't really need your opinions, just the facts. Every detail about the man."

"Well, Sor, it was like this." Haltingly, the private described what he had seen: the Partridges' intransigence; the inclusion of Aspen in the dragnet; the posting of riflemen as a threat; confiscation of the post's trade weapons and other goods; refusal to give the Blackfeet time to dismantle their households; the attempt to capture the children; the torture of Black Wolf and Richard Lamb; the manacles; the arrest of Aspen —Colonel Beeman's eyes darkened at that—the escape of the Indians and then Lamb in the night. . . .

Colonel Beeman had been in the army too long to be outraged by anything, but he was close to that now. He had a practical bent, and even as Murphy talked, Beeman was thinking about ways to undo the damage. Some reports to write, a little discussion with Glenn Ambrose, perhaps court-martial for Partridge, and certainly an official reprimand.

"I'm going to put you on the spot, Murphy. Tell me, privately, whether you think this assignment was well handled. No, I take that back. Forget I asked."

Murphy looked relieved.

The colonel grinned. He had just broken a rule. But he had broken a lot of rules over thirty years.

"Thank you, Private. You may return to your position now, and when you do, please have the sergeant come to me. We'll write out your transfer here and now, and get a copy to you."

"Thank you, Sor. Hope I've been helpful."

They did forty miles that day, and forty the next, and the following day they rode silently up Elk Creek and into Lamb's trading post. The sky was brilliantly blue and the young leaves on the cottonwoods were dancing emeralds. The smell of char assaulted them, and another, sweeter, subtler smell that Beeman instantly recognized with a sinking heart—it was deadly quiet.

Before Barney Beeman's eyes lay the charred remains of Lamb's Post, humped ash upon the earth. A corral and some outbuildings stood. Two wagons sagged forlornly. Far upstream, the lodges stood, empty in the sun without the dance of life around them. There was not a soul any- where, nor an animal.

"Sergeant," he said quietly, "dismount the men, tend the horses, post a sentry on that hill there, and another with the horses. Organize the rest into two-man search details. Start them looking for anything, anything at all, that tells a story to us. Oh, and send Private Murphy to me.

And start the scout reading sign around here."

A moment later, the colonel stared into Private Murphy's face, and saw what he needed to know.

"Private, had this—this carnage—happened before you left?"

"No, Sor. . . I can't imagine. . . ."

"Where were you bivouacked?"

"Here, Sor."

They walked to the encampment area, marked now by the dead ash of a fire, and a few logs. On one log was a stain.

"See those brown stains, Private? Blood, I imagine. Do you make anything of that?"

"Sor, I don't."

"Something terrible happened here, and I intend to find out what."

Around them, horses were being herded and rubbed, men divided and instructed to hunt for anything unusual.

"Is this blood where they tortured Lamb's brother-in-law, what's his name?"

"Black Wolf. No, Sor, that was over to the lodges. Mister Lamb, too, over there."

They walked to the pile of ash that had once been a thriving trading post, almost a village. There was a curious hollow near the southwest corner. Gingerly the colonel trudged through the ash, which swirled up around his shiny boots. In a moment he and Murphy were peering into a stone-lined pit, and seeing heat-twisted barrels of two trade muskets standing in it, along with the ruins of other indecipherable things.

"A cache," the colonel said. "Lamb must have had an ace in the hole under his bedroom for emergencies."

"Nothing left," said Murphy.

There was a shout from a trooper, who was pointing to something or other perched on a corral post. Troopers were congregating there, and staring silently. Barney Beeman strode there, only to be arrested by the sight before him. It was a skull, an Indian skull, eyeless, with bits of rotting flesh hanging from it. A bullet hole pierced the forehead. From the top of it hung glossy black hair, parted at the center and hanging in two braids. Near the bottom of each braid was tied a red, red ribbon.

Beeman groaned. He had a pretty good idea whose skull it was. Grief rose to his throat. "My God, Aspen Lamb!" he muttered, transfixed by the sight.

"Find the rest of her, if there is any," he snapped, scattering blue-shirted troopers in every direction.

There was another cry, this time from within the charred ruin. A trooper pointed at a burned body there, mostly blackened bones now, with a few remnants of fried flesh. The colonel stared. It was impossible to know who this was. The sight was ghastly.

"Private, who was a prisoner in here? Who was being kept in here?"

"Missus Lamb, and her brother, Sor, Black Wolf I think the name was."

"Why was he here?"

"Arrested for resistin' the army, Sor."

"Could this be Lamb himself?"

"Not as I know, Sor. He wasn't in here ever."

"Looks like they burned him alive in here."

Down by the creek now there was another hullabaloo, and one trooper was on his knees, retching. Beeman trotted that way, through brush, and into a sweet noxious stink, and found himself gaping at the headless remains of Aspen Lamb. Predators had torn most of the flesh from her, but there was that creamy doeskin dress, a dress he knew because she always wore it for ceremonial occasions, and had proudly shown it once to him.

"Sergeant," he said huskily. "Prepare a proper grave. A grave fit for a queen, Sergeant. . . . And prepare a marker with the name *Aspen Lamb* burned on it."

Barney Beeman needed to be alone. There were troopers sifting through the post and the lodges upstream, as well as the creek brush and the out-buildings. So he walked east, out upon the sunny horse pasture, and settled down into the grass. It was beautiful here, with the shimmering wall of the Crazy Mountains off to the south and west, and the noble cottonwoods comforting the creek.

It was Eden here, Eden before the Tempter had come. He knew why Lamb had settled here. It hadn't been for business or economic reasons, but something more, something like what he felt peering out of his headquarters window across the shining grasses of the Gallatin valley to the high free mountains beyond.

It was then that the sergeant approached hesitantly, carrying a Bible.

"Found it beneath the largest cottonwood, blood on the grass surrounding it. We dug a bullet from the bark, about the height of her head, Sir."

"Partridge executed her," Beeman muttered. "Stuck her up against that tree and shot her like some criminal. Probably thought he was doing the world a favor, getting rid of one more redskin," he muttered to himself. "And then he cut off her head."

The sergeant said, "There's more, Sir."

Barney Beeman sighed and stood up. His hope for a few moments of seclusion had vanished.

"Yes?"

"Two fresh graves over on the far side of Captain Partridge's bivouac area. A plank at the head of each. Names pencilled in. The best they could do, I imagine. Two infantrymen, Sir. A Moriarty Fiske, and an Armand Ernst."

"Write those names down for me, please. Anything else?"

"That's all for the moment, Sir."

"Thank you, Sergeant, thank you."

Two dead soldiers? Beeman was puzzled now. What had happened here? Some kind of battle, it seemed. Two dead soldiers, one executed trader's wife, one burned body in the ashes, and some blood on that log. Maybe some injured, too.

Heavily he trudged through the pile of ash, looking for further clues. And clues there were, once he began kicking at the black debris: one, then another, and finally a dozen warped, blackened barrels of old flintlocks and caplocks. Aspen's brother had probably waged a one-man war, and the post had probably been burned to get him.

He was beginning to get some idea now of what had transpired here. But one thing was lacking: motive. He had no idea why all this had happened. Surely there was more to it than Partridge ambition? Or was there?

Some while later, his half-Blackfeet scout, Lame Cooke, reported.

"Lotsa tracks, hard to make 'er out," he said, dismounting from a well-lathered chestnut horse.

Beeman nodded. One needed patience with the buck-skinned oldster who circled around what he wanted to say, even as he circled around the things he read on the trail.

It took Lame Cooke several minutes to get to it, but eventually Beeman learned that a small party on shod mounts—army, no doubt—had headed west up the Musselshell. Sometime prior to that an unshod and shod horse, just two, had cut north from the river and headed into the Belt mountains. And there had been a heavy traffic of unshod horses and travois to the southwest, into the Crazies.

Barney Beeman sifted through what he knew and surmised what had happened. The old warrior-mind, the old Indian-fighter instincts, were all at work, shrewdly putting it all together. It was a kind of thinking that had made his career long and successful.

Lamb's Piegans, up in the Crazies, he would not worry about nor would he send his platoon helter-skelter after them. Let them come back when their fear subsided, or let them go up to Badger Creek to report to the Agency. . . . But those two horses cutting north into the Belts, those were a real mystery. There was little he could do about them, for now. What he wanted most was to corral Partridge, who was heading west on the Mussel-shell. He would have to cut north on the Smith if he was returning to Fort Shaw—or chasing Lamb's Piegans. Camp Baker was up there, but it had no telegraph, and was occupied by mules and foot soldiers. Still. . . .

At his field desk he drafted an order, and made a spare copy, just for the record:

A.M., 6-24-77. Captain Partridge, abandon all pursuit. Repeat, abandon all pursuit. Bivouac at Baker, or on Smith River. Am following. Wait for me.—Beeman, Col. USA.

Then he chose a seasoned trooper, Gallant Weatherby, and sent him off with a spare mount.

"Follow their trail if you can read it, Private Weatherby. Catch them if you possibly can. You might well prevent bloodshed if you get there in time. You're over two days behind, but I think you can reach them up near the Missouri if you press. We'll be along behind. And confidentially, Private, if you do find Partridge, be prepared for anything. Use your judgment."

The colonel thought about what he was going to have to tell Richard Lamb, and his chest felt weighted.

"Sergeant," he said, "mount the men."

# CHAPTER 13

For two days they had ridden down an enormous coulee, always northwesterly, angling ever closer to the Smith River and the Missouri. High in the Little Belt mountains it began as a great gash, heavily forested, but this day the pine forests had thinned and they had ridden between great dry grassy slopes, rocky in places, and covered with thin vegetation.

Now, late in the afternoon, they had ridden out

upon the broad valley of the Smith, perhaps a dozen miles from its junction with the Missouri. Less than thirty miles to the northwest, on Sun River, stood Fort Shaw, but Lamb took care not to let Peter Partridge know that. The New York newsman had no idea where he was, and was totally dependent on the old man in this wilderness. Too, over the past week he had seemed to accept his present circumstances, and after two or three surly days he had become helpful and even talkative, asking questions, storing away a dozen stories in his head.

Lamb halted his medicine horse as the broad expanse of the river valley hove into view at the end of a ridge. He had always surveyed open country before emerging from cover. It was a law of life in the wilderness. So he studied the great gray green sea of grass and sagebrush, looking for movement, testing the fresh air for smoke, studying the horizons for the glint of metal. His vision was blurred when he looked at distant prospects, and that continued to bother him.

"What a great empty place. Almost chilling," said Peter.

Lamb smiled. In recent days Peter had started to see things his city-eyes had formerly missed. Deer, for example. Today, a band of antelope. Four days earlier, a wild turkey, which Lamb had promptly shot, even without the benefit of a scattergun. The target might be blurred, Lamb thought, but his aiming instincts held true.

Quietly he led them out upon the open valley and within a mile they struck the Smith, running in oxbows here, between deep cutbanks. They were alone on a sea of prairie. Methodically Lamb studied the ground, looking for marks of passage. There were none. He followed a game trail down a bank and into the river, which ran deep here. He walked the medicine horse, its belly wet, to the west side and continued his careful study of the earth, especially the worn river trail. Then he pushed west another half a mile, found nothing, and returned. Peter Partridge rode with him silently, absorbing whatever lessons Lamb chose to teach.

There were no signs of Lamb's kin. They had not passed here. Maybe they never would; maybe they had fled somewhere. He had ridden hard to get here, pressing Peter to his city-bred limits, making camp in the very last light of June and breaking camp even before the northern sunlight lanced along the wilderness slopes.

He led Peter back to the coulee, where they could watch the traffic along the Smith from some concealment. That night he built the cookfire in a little notch in the slopes, where the flame light would be caught and held by the roll of the earth in almost any direction. They were within the area routinely patrolled by Fort Shaw now, and an encounter would be, at the very least, unfortunate. There were antelope steaks that night from a fine buck Lamb had dropped midafternoon.

Lamb knew, now, what he intended to do. Or at least what he hoped to do, given life's vagaries. First and foremost, he hoped to hook up again with his people, with Hope and Faith and their husbands, and his grandchildren and kin. Next, he would lead them in a wide arc around Fort Shaw, west or east, he didn't know which. Because of the dispatch rider Partridge had sent, there could only be trouble there.

Lamb munched happily on a slice of antelope haunch. The prairie goat was gamey, but filling and nourishing.

There was still a long way to go, he thought. Until a year or so ago, the Blackfoot Agency had been on the Teton River, not far north of Fort Shaw. But then it had been moved up to Badger Creek, further toward Canada. Land-hunger had caused that. The Territory's representatives had beleaguered Congress to shrink the reservation, and now the line ran along Birch Creek, which left the Teton River Agency entirely out of the reservation. And so the new Agency had been built, in the shape of a fort, with an inner yard, on Badger Creek, another fifty miles north.

It galled Lamb to have to scurry there, but once his people were there, they'd be safe. He and Aspen and the girls could visit with friends, endure the winter, and return in the spring to his post, after the army calmed down.

"We must be close to Fort Shaw," Peter said.

Lamb considered a moment, and then replied, "Ye'r right. It's a day's ride northwest."

Peter stared. "Why are you telling me?"

"Because ye've had a chance to think and see for a few days, and ye've been learning about things."

"I could make a break for it tonight."

"So ye could, and likely drown in the Missouri. Two hundred yards of ice water fresh off the peaks. It's not a thing for a tenderfoot."

Peter admitted ruefully, "I have learned to respect your warnings."

Lamb covertly watched the young man. A few days in the wilderness had taken the starch out of him. The arrogance had slowly faded into some sort of resignation.

"What's going to happen next?" the newsman asked.

"We'll wait for my people."

"How do you know they'll come here? This is a sea of wilderness."

"Only two ways to get where they're going, really. This way, or over east, around the Belts and through the Judith Basin."

"I think that's the way we came. We took a ferry across the Missouri at Fort Benton."

Lamb stood, and wandered up to the ridge-top where he could see across the Smith valley.

Nothing stirred in the summer twilight. It would be eleven or so until full dark, and then he'd worry some about them passing in the night.

"How'd you come to marry into an Indian tribe?" Peter asked. He seemed to want to talk this evening.

"Are ye fixing to interview me for one of ye'r newspaper dispatches? Or maybe to polish up those charges ye'r planning on making at Fort Shaw?"

"I . . . just curious."

"I suppose I'll tell ye if ye want to know. But first I'll tell ye why ye'll be a laughing stock if ye accuse me of running guns to the hostiles over in Dakota. The fact is, the Sioux and the Cheyenne don't trade at my post. It's much too far west. And there's no way the ones I trade with, Crow, Blackfeet, and sometimes others, are going to trade weapons—especially repeaters—to their old enemies. Army knows that. Army knows me, too, and for a long time. If ye want to make a fool of ye'rself, go right ahead."

Peter reddened.

"And do ye think the soldiers would try me and throw me in the brig? Ye know better than that. Does it escape ye that I'm a civilian? I've been looking forward to Fort Shaw, if ye want to know. To see ye make a monkey of ye'rself."

"Those dispatches . . . ," the newsman said, unhappily.

Lamb let him stew a little. Then, "When I first laid eyes on Aspen she was a young one—and she was the prettiest thing I ever did see.

"That's not her whole name, ye know. It's Yellow Aspen Leaves Falling, but I never could get my mouth around all that, so she's Aspen. She's the daughter of a headman, that old gent ye met at my post, Singing Bird. He was headman of the Small Robes band—there's ten, twelve bands of Piegan. Not the big chief, like Little Plume is now.

"Well, there she was, shining eyes flashing on me, just like she is now—hardly aged at all, to my way of thinking. And I think maybe she set her feather for me because all the while I was at Singing Bird's lodge, trading robes, there she was, waiting on me, hand and foot.

"I was getting on, forty-five that year, and I thought if I was ever to take a wife, I'd better be at it."

"So you bought her. That's how they do it, isn't it?"

"Not rightly, lad. Indian marriage isn't a buying and selling business. It's more an exchange of property to set up the new household. Like a dowry. The young man, no matter whether he's white or Piegan, offers wealth—horses, rifles, robes in particular. But that's not the end of it. The bride's family offers things too—a lodge, or parfleches, or kitchen things."

"You have no regrets that you didn't marry one of your own kind?"

Lamb grinned. "Aspen and I . . . we've had the best life I could ask for. Or she could ask for, I think."

Some excitement seemed to animate Peter. "Is it true that you were a professor at Amherst College once?"

Lamb eyed him, wondering where he'd heard that. Not that it was any secret. "Academy. It was Amherst Academy then, not College. Yes, I taught classics and antiquities."

"Why did you leave?"

"I suppose ye'r wanting to know if I was in trouble. Maybe use that against me at Fort Shaw, eh?"

Peter flinched.

"Sorry to disappoint ye, lad. But I left because my blood was boiling over. I was young and alive and I couldn't live in a dull gray world full of cobwebs. Sorry, lad, but I bolted out of there for no other reason than to go to the edge of the world, go beyond the rim of civilization. I knew enough about civilizations, ours and the ancient ones, but nothing at all about the savage life, the wild, the free, the place where a man is his own lord, and wears no collar, and survives or not according to his ability."

"So you turned your back on your people and embraced barbaric ones instead."

Lamb fixed him with his eye, long and hard, until the newsman turned away.

"I'll grant that all this may seem barbaric to ye," he replied gently. "These are people who used stone tools, had no iron, didn't know the wheel, still live in skin lodges like nomads. A fierce people, too. Take scalps, torture and mutilate prisoners. Worship animal spirits and totems—as well as the God we know. They call him Old Man, Napi. The Creator. Know what they call white men? Napikwan, Old Man Person. Ye see, Napi, Old Man, is something of a trickster. Does that tell ye anything?

"Barbaric, ye say. Well, I'll tell ye, in some ways they are more civilized than ye are. And their religion is a serious, sacred thing. And the headman makes sure the poorest in the band, the widows, have meat and a lodge."

The newsman was not impressed. "All very pretty, and sentimental, Lamb. The noble savage. But still the savage."

Richard Lamb chose silence. He stared at the remaining embers of the cookfire, and then out upon the night. Something cautioned him that Peter Partridge was more obtuse than ever—and more dangerous.

"I'm going to turn in, but I'll tell ye something first, Mr. Newsman. Ye have more to lose at Fort Shaw than I do. Ye and ye'r brother have reputations to lose, and ambitions to be frustrated, and integrity to be lost—if it hasn't been already. And a lot more. Ye can take nothing of the sort from me. Do ye understand?"

"No. We always come out ahead. We have the power to do so."

"That's what I thought, lad."

The medicine horse whickered gently and he was instantly awake. Richard Lamb had spent a lifetime with horses in camp, and knew a friendly greeting when he heard one. The night breeze out of the west had carried its message to the spotted stallion.

He saddled swiftly. Partridge was either asleep or feigning it. There was no moon, but the night was clear and dry and starlit. He sprang easily to the saddle—the toil of the last days had hardened his old muscles—and rode out of the coulee.

In a few minutes he was among them, and clutching Hope and Faith to him, and clasping the warm hands of Turtle and Standing Bear, and throwing an arm over the young shoulder of his grandson Bigtooth Beaver, and slipping a big rough hand into the little one of shy Pawing Horse, Faith's daughter. Beside him the big medicine horse glowed eerily in the dark, a beacon of his presence.

"Now let me have the news," he said in his rough Blackfeet tongue. "Is everyone here and well? Is Aspen here, or Black Wolf?"

"They are at the post," Faith replied. "But the rest of us are here. Grandmother and Grandfather have come this far. They are very tired."

Standing Bear said, "The horses are very weary, and we have no spares. We lost one. It went lame. So we are burdening the others even more."

Lamb said, "Ye are travelling at night. Why is that?"

Turtle chose to answer. "I have been riding rear guard," he said. "The bluebellies are only half a day behind us now, and gaining. Our horses are worn and overloaded. And we have old people and children to think of. So this night we continued, even though it is killing our ponies."

Standing Bear said, "We hope to cross the Missouri and then rest a day or two."

"It's a bad time to cross the river," Lamb said. "Turtle, have you actually seen the soldiers?"

"Several times. There are eight. The bluebelly chief and seven more."

"And not Aspen?"

"Our mother is not with them."

Lamb pondered. "Seven, eh? One was sent to Fort Ellis. Two may be back there at the post, looking after Aspen and Black Wolf and the property. That makes sense. Have ye fought? Have ye skirmished? Did ye try for their horses?"

"We could have taken their horses many times," Turtle said with contempt. "But we have been true to your command, Father, and have avoided war. We have not given the bluebellies any reason to shoot."

"That's good," Lamb said. "Turtle, can ye tell me how far they are in miles?"

"I do not know miles. If they had fresh horses, and ran them hard, they could be here in two hours. But their horses are as worn as ours."

"So little time." Lamb mulled a moment. "Are ye hungry?"

"We have not eaten for a day," said Faith. "The children bear it bravely. There has not been time except to boil some bone marrow broth."

"I can feed ye a little. I have a fresh antelope hanging. Not much for all of ye, but a bit, and we had only a little."

"We?" asked Turtle.

"I have the captain's brother, the one in short pants, a prisoner."

"Why is that? Isn't that a danger to us?"

Lamb sighed. "The soldier chief, Partridge, was threatening Aspen. I took the brother to make sure he doesn't threaten very hard."

Hope said, "But the captain is mad. I saw madness in his face. Are you sure . . . ?"

"No, not sure. Best I could manage," Lamb said shortly. "Gave me a chance to talk with the brother, and maybe get his help. Maybe get some sense into him before he writes all the talking signs for the people back East."

Lamb knew, even as he said it, that changing Peter's mind wasn't very likely.

He led them to the mouth of the great coulee, and in for about a hundred yards. Peter sat up with a start, fear upon his face, as he gazed at the angular faces above him in the night.

Swiftly the women added kindling to the remaining embers until a hot fire snapped, and with practiced hands they skinned every bit of flesh from the strung-up antelope and started it roasting. In a small kettle they began a stew for the old people. The silent children each led a horse or two to grass and rubbed the animals as they grazed. The men posted sentries on the dark ridges, and began checking hoofs for pebble bruises.

All this Peter Partridge watched in the flickering firelight, his face a study in amazement and apprehension. Lamb was speaking now in a harsh strange tongue, and Partridge seemed to be virtually forgotten. But it did not escape him that these were people in hard flight, people who were running in the night.

Lamb approached at last. "We'll be travelling shortly. Get ye'r horse saddled," he said brusquely.

Peter caught his army mount and cinched down the McClellan over its horsehair pad. The Indians ignored him; it was as if Peter weren't even there.

The meat was still half-raw when the women began setting slices of it on a sandstone boulder to cool. The children were fed first; then the men, who came in from sentry posts one by one. And, finally, the women. Somehow, the antelope had provided them all with a small, precious meal.

Peter stared at the carcass, now clean-picked bone. The thoroughness amazed him. The women were now cracking bone and extracting marrow. Lamb's daughter, Hope, was dumping that marrow into the broth.

The almost toothless old people, huddled in a buffalo robe, sipped broth from metal cups, even as the women brewed some more.

It had all been done in minutes, and now the fire was extinguished and the horses saddled. They had been here less than an hour.

"We'll lead the horses now," said Lamb. "Except for Grandmother and Grandfather. The rest of us will walk and let these ponies rest. They'll need all the strength they have to swim the Missouri."

The Smith ran north, but he led them northeast, taking his bearings from the North Star. The Missouri dipped a little south ahead, and they would reach it sooner. There were several buffalo crossings up there above the great falls, and he intended to cross at one which was belly-high most of the year. And in cutting east he would begin his great arc around Fort Shaw and its probing patrols. They'd cut the road between the post and Fort Benton, no doubt leaving sign of the passage of about thirty horses, but it could not be helped.

Thus they walked through the moonless night, with the led horses snatching grass, and resting after a fashion. The grandparents clung gamely to the manes of their mounts.

Lamb fell into an easy gait. He was not at all tired. But there was forming in his mind a dread of the river at its icy worst. The risks would be terrible. He supposed Partridge knew that, and might be hoping the Piegans would hesitate on the bank, and be pinned there. But, thought Lamb dourly, the captain had always underestimated the Piegan.

After an hour of walking it occurred to Lamb that he had not seen Peter recently. Lamb pulled aside and let the procession pass in the night. He peered intently into each face. The newsman was gone. No doubt he took his leave in the midst of the hubbub when they started out.

Lamb wondered, for a moment, what direction the man had gone, and guessed south. He doubted that the newsman would try the dangerous river alone, especially after being warned. He must have read the sign—a band of exhausted women and children running in the night could mean only one thing: The soldiers were close behind. Partridge didn't understand the Blackfeet tongue, but he had read the circumstances well enough.

Lamb sighed. There went Aspen's safety. But

maybe it wasn't that bad. Captain Partridge, by all accounts, was now over a hundred miles from Aspen—more like two hundred if you counted the bends of the river. With seven men. So she was safe from his threats for the time being. In fact, the further Captain Partridge rode from the trading post, the better Lamb liked it.

Let the knickerbocker go, he thought. The newsman had served his purpose.

# CHAPTER 14

Eleven miles to the south, on the east bank of the Smith River, Captain Partridge called a halt. His horses were faltering. Three were lame. One was saddle-galled.

These mounted infantry! he raged. How little they knew about horses!

"Rub down those mounts," he commanded. "Check those hoofs. I am going to inspect hoofs in ten minutes."

The soldiers were sour and tired and dirty. Blood had seeped through Private Rudeen's head bandage, and the man looked drawn.

"Pinski," the captain snapped. "Take that saddle pad down to the river and wash it thoroughly. You've galled that horse, ruined an army mount. If it can't be ridden any further, you'll walk."

Private Goldsmith's wounded arm had swollen

until it bulged out his shirtsleeve, but the man was in better shape than Johnny Johnson, who had lost fingers and had a bloody rag tied over his hand.

"Go help Johnson," the captain commanded Goldsmith. "He can't unsaddle one-handed." He turned and said, "Grouard, help these men. Unsaddle that horse and then go out and scout on foot."

The private nodded.

"Private, what do you say when you're spoken to by an officer?"

"Yes, Sir," Grouard muttered.

Because of Grouard's earlier scouting, the captain knew the hostiles were perhaps ten miles ahead, and that he was swiftly gaining on them. If these horses could last another day or so, he might still catch the hostiles at the river. In the water they'd be sitting ducks, swimming slowly. He hoped Lamb was with them.

There had been no fresh army mounts at Camp Baker, only a few pack mules and privately owned officers' horses. That had disappointed him because he had been counting on the fresh animals.

Partridge began a methodical examination of his mounts: He found a pebble wedged next to the frog of the off hind hoof of Goldsmith's horse; the knees of several were hot and swollen.

In a rage, he snarled, "Turn them out to pasture. If you've ruined good army mounts you'll all walk and you'll all carry your saddles and gear. We're going to catch those Piegans either mounted or on foot. They're only two or three hours ahead of us now—or would be if our horses were fresh."

The captain brushed his own fine mount furiously. The bay was in better shape than the others, perhaps because Partridge had grown up with horses in Albany and knew how to ride them without exhausting them.

There'd be only field rations tonight. Hardtack and jerky. They hadn't had a decent meal in days. No game. An army horse column was so noisy it scared off anything within miles.

"Rudeen, look to the wounded. If there's carbolic in the field surgery, use it. And fresh dressings."

"Yes, Sir," the former corporal mumbled.

The men had collapsed in the grass, not bothering with food.

"You all stink," the captain said. "I want you to wash your shirts right now. And the rest of your clothing, for that matter. And while you're at it, I want every saddle pad or saddle blanket washed."

"What'll we sleep in, Sir?" asked Rudeen.

"Your skin. It's warm enough."

He did not have to wash his own shirt because he had a spare.

Wearily, the men scrubbed their clothes and the saddle blankets and wrung them out. Rudeen artfully draped his things over sticks near a little coffee fire he had going, and the others did the same. As the stretching twilight turned to night, some of the chilled men put their damp clothing back on. It was better than cold night breezes.

None of the men had forgotten the events at Lamb's Post, nor had they forgotten they were all facing serious charges when they returned to Fort Shaw. Mutiny was a grave offense. Even though they were exhausted, they knew they would not sleep much. By dawn they would be badly chilled. Rudeen was aware of this, and slowly gathered a pile of dry wood for the fire.

Near midnight, Barney Beeman's dispatch rider, Gallant Weatherby, rode in. He was unchallenged because no sentries had been posted.

The captain awoke with a start. It was very dark, and a man on a horse loomed above him like a great shadow.

"I have a dispatch for Captain Partridge," said an unfamiliar voice in the night. "Is he here?"

"I am Partridge."

The man dismounted. The captain saw now that there was a second horse, and that both animals had been ridden hard.

"Dispatch from Colonel Beeman, Fort Ellis, for you, Sir. I'm Weatherby."

"You're what, soldier?"

"Private Weatherby, Sir; Fort Ellis."

Partridge wondered, "How could Beeman possibly know where—"

The flickering fire wouldn't do. He dug into his kit for a candle, and when at last he had light, took the proffered dispatch and read.

"Stop here? Let these hostiles go?" He studied the impassive face of the dispatch rider. "Private, where were you sent from? Ellis?"

"No, Lamb's Post."

*"Lamb's Post!"* He read the order again. "Why?"

"I wouldn't know, Sir."

"Beeman could see we lost men there. Why's he calling a halt?"

The rider said nothing, his eyes averted.

Partridge grinned suddenly. "Take care of your mounts, Trooper. Maybe there's coffee left in that pot. We have only field rations. Oh, one more question—where's Beeman now?"

"Behind me, Sir. I don't know how far."

"All right. Dismissed. I may have instructions for you shortly."

The soldiers stared at the captain, curious. He blew out the candle. "Get your rest," he snapped.

In the flickering firelight Joe Partridge's mind seethed. He hated taking orders from Beeman rather than his own CO. Hated being stopped at the gates of success. What was Beeman up to? Maybe there was a way around Beeman's order. That is what army life was all about—getting around obstacles. He'd always gotten around them. It was a Partridge tradition. Like becoming a lieutenant. When the army refused him a commission during the war, his father had talked to a few politicians and that was that. When Peter had gotten kicked out of the academy back in Albany for trifling with the headmaster's daughter, a little endowment from the Partridge family changed everything. Maybe he could commandeer those two horses brought by the dispatch rider. They'd been used hard, but were fresher than his own mounts. . . .

A little before dawn a rider approached camp from the north, oblivious of the cocking weapons of men who heard him come.

"Is this Captain Partridge's command?" asked a voice that was instantly familiar to Joseph, in his bedroll.

"Peter!" he shouted.

The soldiers, awakened, stared stonily.

"Rudeen! Build up that fire."

The former corporal, whose revolver had been cocked and pointed at the shadowed intruder, slid the hammer forward and rolled out. So did the others. There'd be no more rest.

Peter was a sight, Joseph thought. His face bristled with stubble; the brown knickers were filthy; the jacket a ruin. The argyle stockings tumbled around his calves.

"You're safe! And free! How'd you get here?"

"I got away from the old renegade up the trail. He's not far ahead, you know. He hooked up with his Indian kin tonight, and I slipped away during all that. . . . You can catch 'em, Joe. They were done for, pushing along at night. I knew that meant you weren't far behind. So I waited my chance while they ate, and here I am. I—you'll be proud of me, Joe—I didn't just light out. I slipped out to the river brush and waited in the dark to see which way they'd go. And it was a good thing, because they left the river and started northeast."

"Northeast?" The captain thought about that. "Probably making a wide circle around the fort."

In a few minutes Joseph had Peter's story. But Peter found the captain reluctant to talk much about what had happened at Lamb's Post. Eventually he was told that there had been a fight; the captain had lost two men, with three more injured; and Lamb's brother-in-law had been killed.

"Who's that?" Peter asked, pointing at the cavalry trooper.

"Dispatch rider from Beeman at Fort Ellis. I've been ordered to abandon pursuit and wait in place."

That occasioned another bombardment of questions from Peter, ones that Joe couldn't very well answer.

"I don't understand it," Peter muttered. "You've got wounded that need care, and now you're stuck here."

That was it, the thing Joe Partridge had been reaching at in his mind.

"Trooper," he called to the cavalryman, who

211

was sipping coffee. Private Gallant Weatherby stood and approached.

"Sir?"

"Please give Colonel Beeman my regards. Please tell him that I am abandoning the pursuit as directed, but am proceeding to Fort Shaw at once with three wounded men. Now repeat that back to me."

Weatherby did.

"You are free to leave when ready. There's no urgency, Trooper. Spare your mounts."

A few minutes later the cavalryman rode south, with his spare mount jogging behind him.

Peter frowned. "You giving up the chase?"

"Not at all. Following orders. I'm heading for Fort Shaw now, and then we'll catch the Piegans and Lamb on the other side. They'll lose about two days making that circle. That was good reconnoitering, Peter. At any rate, I want to tell the story to Ambrose my own way, before Beeman gets there and muddies the water. And then, with a fresh command—a whole company if Ambrose'll let me—I can catch the hostiles and nail Lamb."

The captain smiled.

The newsman grinned. "You know, being held hostage by him wasn't any loss. I got that old renegade to talking, and now I've got some great stories to write. He's tough, Joe. I admire the old trapper, in a way."

"Forget it. We're turning him over to federal

authorities for destroying army property—and for anything else I can think to throw at him. He's done for. His life is over."

They struck northwest, straight for the fort, negotiating the river at a favorite army ford below Little Muddy Creek. By evening mess, the fort was in sight. Two hours later the weary horses, which had not faltered these last thirty miles, plodded in.

Colonel Glenn Ambrose was waiting.

"Beeman relayed your request for reinforcements," he said. "The wire requested help in locating and escorting Lamb's Blackfeet. Tell me about it, Captain. Tell me everything, because it doesn't make a bit of sense. All this over a few friendly trading-post Indians."

Partridge was uncomfortable before this short, thin, baggy-eyed, wax-mustached CO. His career, his ambitions, rode on what he would say now. He had deaths to account for. But all the way back from the Smith River, he had rehearsed for this moment, anticipating the man's questions as ruthlessly as a trial lawyer anticipates the responses of a hostile witness. He'd planned to put a good face on it, and if all else failed, there was always the Partridge family influence.

"You see, Sir, Lamb's Post was a nest of hostiles. No one suspected it. We certainly didn't, coming peaceably to execute policy. Did you know, Glenn, that there was a large traffic of arms and ammunition to the hostiles? Right there, and we didn't even suspect. Well, I lost two men, and three wounded—they're over at the surgery now —but perhaps I've saved the army hundreds of lives and a lot of grief."

The CO eyed him skeptically.

"Now let me explain. . . ."

It took a half hour.

Ambrose stared at the ceiling. "Why did you include Mrs. Lamb in your dragnet? What earthly reason was there for bringing Lamb's wife up here?"

"Following orders, Glenn. You know instructions were—"

"You had leeway, Captain. We all have leeway, some discretion. In fact, you properly exercised that discretion, bringing the wounded here, rather than obeying Beeman's order to wait in place. Now why did you include Mrs. Lamb?"

"She was . . . a hostile, Colonel."

"Hardly. Now why do you suppose Colonel Beeman intervened?"

"I can't imagine, Glenn. It's tragic. That band should be caught and punished for killing army men, and Lamb brought to heel."

Something glittered in the CO's eyes. "How did you say she died, again?"

"During the fight, Glenn. She emerged from the post and was shot."

"She was shot, was she? I'll pursue that later. I plan to question your men."

"The men are not reliable witnesses, Glenn. They mutinied, and I will begin proceedings at once for that and a variety of other matters. I've never commanded such a bunch of cowards and fools."

The colonel sniffed a cigar and bit off the end. "We have good men. I trained many of them myself. Now tell me again about Lamb. I don't understand why he abducted your brother. It makes no sense at all."

"Leverage, Glenn. He supposed he could intimidate me, cow the army, by taking a hostage. I proved him wrong."

"You haven't told me why an old man would take such desperate measures, Captain." Ambrose lit his cigar and puffed.

"He's a renegade. A law unto himself, Glenn."

"Your story doesn't make a hell of a lot of sense, Partridge. Now I've got men dead, men injured, some friendlies running, a trader's wife and kin dead, his post burned, the man himself and his family on the run . . . and maybe charged with abducting a civilian. I've also got Colonel Beeman sending dispatches telling you to stop, and marching toward here fast . . . and God knows what else."

"It'll make sense when you hear my brother's side. And Colonel Beeman will confirm what I've told you."

Glenn Ambrose stood. "You have the freedom of the post but not beyond. I want you on hand for more questioning. Dismissed, Captain."

"But, Sir. . . ."

"Yes?"

"We can catch them. They're circling around here. I can catch them due north of here, when they swing back. . . ."

"Why *should* we intercept them? Aren't they going where we wanted them to go? And all on their own? To their reservation, as you requested?"

"I didn't request. I ordered them. And they're hostiles now, Sir. *Hostiles*. They killed two men and injured others. And Lamb is with them. Are you just going to let them escape punishment?"

Ambrose sighed. "You're staying here. I'm not going to send you out with a fresh command after Barney ordered you not to pursue."

"But Glenn . . . ah, Sir. . . ."

"He'll be along directly. I'll decide what to do after I talk with him. Please do not leave this post, Captain Partridge."


A few minutes later, Private Rudeen was standing before Colonel Ambrose.

"At ease, Private. I'm sorry to pull you from the surgery. How is your head?"

"It hurts, Sir, but I'll be fine soon."

"That's good." The CO tugged at his waxed mustache. "I want you to tell me the entire story, every detail, as accurately as you know how. No opinions, just facts."

Rudeen looked reluctant. "I'm in trouble, Sir . . . I don't know how. . . ."

Ambrose blazed. "You may or may not be in trouble at all. I'll decide that. If you're afraid to talk—to tattle—about an officer, forget it. I'll get that story one way or another, and I'll protect you from the consequences if I can. You're one of the best men I've got, so I want to hear what happened from you."

"I face mutiny charges, Sir. I'd rather not."

"Maybe you do and maybe you don't. I can't help you until I know the whole story."

Glenn Ambrose had to drag it out of the soldier, but eventually he got most of it. After Rudeen had finished, the colonel said, "Now tell me about this alleged mutiny."

"Well, Sir, the captain was threatening to execute Mrs. Lamb, and we knew he'd make us do it."

"Execute? *Execute?* He told me Mrs. Lamb emerged from the post and was shot."

"We couldn't stomach it, Sir. It looked like, uh, murder. So they asked me, since I was the corporal, to petition. . . ."

"And the captain denied the petition?"

"Yes. He said it was none of our business and we must follow orders. So then I told him we would all prefer the stockade rather than shoot that woman, and he said that was mutiny, and we were in trouble."

"Did you threaten him?"

"No, Sir."

Ambrose was pensive. "You say you all preferred the stockade and told him so? You were saying you'd accept army discipline in the matter?"

"Yes, Sir."

"Some mutiny. All right, then. Tell me about this execution."

"The captain forced some men at gunpoint to go get Mrs. Lamb. They got her and led her to a tree. He ordered them to fire. They did, but not at her. He was angry and cursed the men and walked up and shot her with his revolver."

"Why? Why did he execute her?"

"After the Piegan escaped and Lamb returned, he told Lamb he'd shoot her—he had her under guard in the post—unless Lamb brought the Blackfeet back."

"But weren't they going to the reservation? Why bring them back?"

"He told Lamb he intended to escort the Indians there."

Ambrose pondered that. It was coming clear now. "And so Lamb grabbed the brother, the newsman, as a hostage to protect Mrs. Lamb. Is that about it? Who threatened to shoot a hostage first?"

"The captain, Sir. He told Lamb to bring back the Piegans or he'd shoot her, and the other Indian too."

Ambrose was silent for a long time. Then, "Why'd he bust you to private?"

"For the mutiny, as he called it, and I don't know what all. He didn't like the way I handled things after Lamb took Peter Partridge. I did pursue for an hour or so, but we lost them."

"I want your opinion, now, and I'll hold it in strictest confidence. Do you think the newsman's presence in any way affected the situation?"

Rudeen hesitated. "He . . . caused trouble, Sir. Always egging on the captain. He seemed to have—ah, well, a blood-and-thunder idea of chasing Indians. I heard them talking. He was going to write stories, the captain would be a hero. . . ."

"Thank you, Rudeen. I'm getting some sense of all this now. Will the other enlisted men talk?"

"They are very frightened of the charges, Sir."

"I'll speak to them. Go on back to the sick ward and get your rest. You're on better ground than you know—if your story is true."

One by one, Ambrose probed the others, all of them frightened and wary of saying anything. But everything he got from them confirmed what Rudeen had said.

Now he'd wait for Barney Beeman. If Beeman had examined the ruins carefully he could confirm either Partridge or Rudeen and the others. One or the other side, but not both.

He frowned. He couldn't prevent Partridge from filing charges and starting court-martial. That was his privilege. But maybe . . . just maybe . . . if Partridge filed charges, he would take a step too far.

The next day Colonel Barnabas Beeman rode in, with twenty cavalrymen.

# CHAPTER 15

At sunrise they were at the Missouri. It was wider here at the crossing, and the slopes to either side were gentle. Lamb had crossed here once during his trapping days. He studied the turbid cold river with mounting dread. It was not running at its spring peak, but neither had it settled back to its quiet summer flow.

His people were weary and the horses were listless. They had trudged uncomplainingly through the long night with little rest. At dawn, Turtle reported that they were no longer being pursued; the bluebellies had steered toward Fort Shaw. That gave them a chance to rest in the cool sun.

In the riverbrush, Standing Bear had scared up a doe and shot it. That was good, Lamb thought. Let us eat and rest; let the ponies graze and recover their strength. Then the river would seem less formidable. And so they cooked and ate, and let the unburdened horses roll in a buffalo wallow, and spread out upon the rich young grass.

He squatted down beside Grandfather Singing Bird and Grandmother Prairie Dog Song, and in their tongue asked them how they fared.

"We are tired in the bones, Son, but the day is sunny and we will be warm. If we should fail to get across the great river, do not wait. We are home wherever we are, and no great harm will befall us," said the old man.

"I know ye are home here, Father, but soon there will be a warm lodge for ye, and a good stew every day."

He wasn't really sure of that, but they smiled.

"Don't come asking for more daughters," teased the old woman.

Lamb paused at the small hot fire Faith had built. Thinly sliced venison haunch roasted over it on green spits. Solemnly, with patient brown eyes, her three children watched the meat hiss and drip.

Faith was bitter. "Why?" she asked him. "Why do these soldiers pursue us? What have we done? Why couldn't we stay at our post and live the way we always have lived, a friend of all? I'm tired, and very angry, and even if I'm half your blood, I hate the napikwan. I want to go home."

He hunkered down beside her, fixing her with his one good eye.

"We'll go back soon," he replied. "As to why

this happened, some army officers make careers out of chasing and slaughtering the Indian people." He paused a long moment. "Just as some braves and some chiefs have made careers of stealing horses, raiding other tribes, or killing whites. Up until about the time ye were born, Faith, the Piegans were the most warlike of all the northern tribes. A terror to all."

She glanced into her father's face, and grinned. "You're right," she said. "It is life. But I like mother's people better than yours."

She pulled the smoking brown meat off the flame and set it aside to cool. The children watched it expectantly.

He ate with Hope and her family, and then walked restlessly down to the hard, cold water. He guessed the ponies could find bottom well out from here, but they'd still have to swim fifty or seventy yards. Some instinct brought the buffalo here to cross, and Lamb decided it was good to follow their lead. He wished there were some in sight, but the herds had declined, and their doomsday would come soon. The Indians thought the herds had merely gone elsewhere, driven away by enemies, and were as plentiful as ever. But Lamb knew. He knew the toll of the hide-hunters. He knew he had contributed to the decline, trading for robes.

He sighed. When he returned to camp he said to Turtle, "Let us begin."

When everyone reached the river the young man removed his leggings and his elkskin shirt and tied them in a bundle. Then, in only his breechclout, he eased his spotted pony into the swirling water. The reluctant animal balked and then surrendered, the water swirling higher as Turtle edged out. Then suddenly the horse was swimming while the racing water pushed it downstream. It found bottom at last, far across, and far downstream. But it had crossed without mishap. The spotted horse shook himself violently on the far bank, spraying water that glittered in the sun.

He would go next, thought Richard Lamb. He thought to take off his skin clothes that had been so lovingly sewn and decorated by Aspen. But the day was warm and the clothes had been grimed by the trail, so he would let the swirling waters wash them. He edged the tall medicine horse into the water, felt it stride powerfully ahead, felt the icy water sandpaper his ankles and thighs, and then the horse hit the channel and was swimming hard. The brutal water sapped the heat out of both the horse and the old man. But the rhythmic churning of the horse put them across, and when the horse found bottom it lunged ahead in a series of great leaps. Lamb felt numb. He doffed his buckskins and wrung them out while his pale flesh goose-bumped in the warming sun.

Then it was time for Grandfather and Grandmother. Gamely the two old people urged their mounts into the cold water, clinging grimly to the manes. The water sucked around them, once unseating Prairie Dog Song, who canted sideways as water plucked at her. But slowly the old woman righted herself and her horse found bottom and in great leaps was out. Singing Bird's horse followed. The elderly couple trembled blue with cold, and Lamb led them to a warm rock ledge where they could absorb the early sun. They shook uncontrol-lably.

That was the worst of it, he thought, unless the tug of the ice water was too much for any of the smaller children. For one angry moment he thought about Partridge, and the army, and the ordeal the United States government was imposing on his kin for no reason, no reason at all.

They came in bunches now, the women futilely pulling their skirts high up on their bronzed legs, even while knowing that the heavy skin skirts, and a few calico ones, would be soggy with water. The pack horses came too, with water lapping at the bundles and parfleches tied on them and soaking the rolled-up buffalo robes. Children clung to manes and shivered. Here on the north bank, women were wringing water from their heavy clothes.

A shrill cry galvanized him. He glimpsed a child off of a pony, clinging with small hands to its mane while the cruel water boiled around. A moment later the small hands let go and the little one vanished in the hurrying waters. The pony swam toward shore. Far downstream, a dark head bobbed, and was gone again.

The cry had erupted from Faith. He saw her now, urging her pony straight down stream in the middle of the channel. But the horse pawed for the far bank and fought her. Standing Bear, still on the south bank, guarding the rear of the band, saw his wife, saw the child vanish, knew it was their youngest, Laughing Girl, and kicked his fine strong gelding into the water, holding his Henry rifle over his head.

Then, as Richard Lamb watched transfixed, Faith did the unthinkable, the terrible. She abandoned her pony and tried to swim downstream toward the three-year-old girl, who was no longer visible. For a moment or two he could follow Faith in the water, and see her long black hair swirl behind her. But he knew, with sinking soul, that he would never again see her alive. Water like that would swiftly numb her muscles; the doeskin clothes would wrap her like a lead-weighted shroud. The warm girl he had sired and loved was gone.

Standing Bear wrestled his pony to a downstream angle, flailing at it wildly. He dropped his Henry, and with a final glint—like a jumping trout—it vanished. He urged the horse downstream until it weakened dangerously, its powerful muscles numbed.

Lamb, coming alive suddenly, swept up on his medicine horse and raced down the shore. If there was any breath of life in Faith or the child, he'd find it. For half a mile he raced along the shore of the cruel river, squinting into its murky depths, seeing nothing. Then, as he rounded a sweeping curve and a sandbar hove into sight, he saw her form caught on it, the waters still plucking at her legs. He leapt off the horse and knelt, and knew she was dead. He carried her up on the sand, letting water pour from her mouth and nose. He lifted her cold form and hugged her. But she was gone. The river had claimed her. No, not the river, really—the army had taken her, his daughter, and his berry-brown granddaughter.

Standing Bear rode up on a trembling pony, and climbed silently down, and took his wife from Richard Lamb's arms and held her wet cold body close to his own, darkness in his black eyes. Briefly he scanned the river, helplessly looking for the child. Then he wept.

They rode slowly back to the buffalo crossing, with Faith's limp body in Standing Bear's arms, and the pony staggering beneath them. The others stared. Hope cried and ran to her lifeless sister. The rest of the women, in the ancient custom of the Piegan, began to wail softly, keening in the warm June air beneath a golden sun.

They tarried there the rest of that day, silently drying out their things, spreading the soaked buffalo robes upon the green grasses to let the sun steam the water out of them. They wrung out their buckskin clothing and donned such cloth clothes as they had. It was warm, and they needed little.

There was, in a long and gentle coulee nearby, a string of cottonwoods stretching from the river-bank for a quarter of a mile until the coulee ended upon the high plains. Here Turtle and Standing Bear and the others began the solemn task of building a scaffold high in a cottonwood, while Luke Old Coyote stood guard on a nearby knoll. With their trade hatchets they cut straight poles, and these they lashed to crossbars tied to the living tree. It was a sacred business, one to be done with care and reverence, so that Father Sun would welcome the spirit of Faith—Spring Willow— and guide it to the Sandhills.

The women dressed Spring Willow in her finest doeskins, ones she wore only for sacred occasions, such as the summer sun-dance. On the bodice, patterned in large trade beads, were intricate symbols of sun and lightning and the willow tree. The few small possessions of Laughing Girl—a tiny skirt, a gourd rattle—were placed in Faith's hands, and then she was encased in the finest, softest buffalo robe her lodge possessed. The young men carried her to the scaffold and lashed her there with rawhide.

It was a cloudless day, and the azure sky filtered through the leaves and the dark form above them.

There was no medicine man present, so they waited for a word or signal from Richard Lamb. But the old man, his beard white in the filtered sun, had little to say and stood quietly. Simple silence seemed best. Hope stood beside him.

Finally he said, "I commend ye'r soul to God." Then he said it again in the tongue of these people.

A few minutes later he gave the signal to be off. Standing Bear rode alone and quiet far ahead, acting as the advance scout, but wanting to be alone. Faith's children, Bigtooth Beaver and Pawing Horse, clung close to Hope and their cousins. And so the small band rode north once again on a fine day, and at dusk, after a long ride, they made camp in a cottonwood stand beside a creek.

And that is when Grandmother Prairie Dog Song quietly died. The cold of the river had been too much for her, but she had stoically clung to life, upright in her saddle, until it was time to die. She had stepped down from her pony without help, walked to a tree, sat down, and let go. Grandfather Singing Bird found her thus.

"Prepare two scaffolds," said the ancient one, "for I shall join her now and we will begin our long sojourn in the Sandhills."

No one protested, for it was unseemly to ask him to continue when his spirit had told him his time had come. And so again the young men hewed fine straight poles and lashed them carefully until a place for two was wrought in the arms of a young cottonwood tree near the creek. It was no sad thing this time, and no one wailed in the dusk. In the morning, when Father Sun could see this new oblation to him, they lashed the old woman to her resting place and lifted the old man there as well, and gave him the things he would need for his spirit journey—his scalps, his totems, a fine bow and a quiver of iron-tipped arrows. These he arranged around himself, drawing the black buffalo robe around him. He dismissed them with a smile and a glint of joy in his shining eyes.

The only sadness Lamb felt was that Aspen and Black Wolf were not present to say goodbye to their parents. But he memorized the occasion in all its detail so that he might tell them of the parting exactly as he saw it when they were all together again.

They rode north once more through sun-swept high plains verdant with buffalo grass and sweet sage. These were the heartlands of the Blackfeet people now, and the grief they all felt was tempered by the joy of the country that stirred the blood of any Piegan or Siksika or Blood. This was Home.

Lamb felt these things too, but he was not as affected by them as his kin. His mind turned, rather, on the sadness of this journey that had been forced upon them for no valid purpose; a journey from somewhere to somewhere to please distant generals in a blue army who penned abstract orders and thought not at all of the realities they entailed.

About midafternoon on that sun-drenched day the widower Standing Bear rode swiftly back to his kin a mile or so behind him. Directly, he rode to Richard Lamb with his news: "There is a great Piegan camp over the brow of that low ridge," he said, pointing northeast. "Two hundred lodges at least. Maybe three hundred, I cannot tell. They have found buffalo and are in the midst of a great hunt."

The news startled Lamb. "Are ye sure they are the People?" he asked. He used the word *kainah*, Many Chiefs, which is what all the Blackfeet called themselves.

"I am sure. The lodges are none other."

The news flew electrically through these kin of Richard Lamb, and they veered a few compass points east of the direction they had travelled. When they topped the low ridge they were amazed. It was exactly as Standing Bear had said: Skin lodges, too many to count, with fire-blackened tops and golden buffalo cowhide stretching out below, dotted a broad green valley. Everywhere fresh hides were staked out to dry. Others being fleshed by women at the lodges. To the north was a great herd of ponies. Smoke curled lazily from a few lodges but most of the women were cooking on fires in front of their lodges rather than inside. On pole racks, great quantities of thin-sliced meat were drying into jerky. The men of the camp were off on the hunt, but now a host of boys and old men rode swiftly toward the ridge where Lamb's people stood, and exchanged greetings in the tongue that bound them together as a tribe and a band.

From one proud youth they learned that this great camp was led by Little Plume himself, chief of all the Piegans. Lamb led his people down the long gentle slope, a joyous reunion and home-coming following so close on the death of their loved ones. Everywhere was the evidence of the camp's recent success—drying meat, rich light summer robes being tanned, hanging hump-meat, and dogs revelling in the offal.

They rode amid the clamor and the cries of cousins and kin to the largest lodge, the home of Little Plume. It was richly adorned with geometric designs in gold and azure representing the sun and sky. Before the lodge was a tripod bearing a dozen scalps and a feather-bedecked weasel skin trimmed with red tradecloth.

The chief was waiting for them. He wore only a breech-clout and the traditional high black moccasins of his people. The sharp planes of his face were framed by iron-black hair laced with gray, and the hard, rippling muscles of his chest and shoulders bore the scars of battle and torture.

"The trader Lamb and his kin," he said in his own tongue. "We are happy you are here. The buffalo are plentiful to the east, and you will share the hunt with us."

Lamb dismounted stiffly and was ushered into the great lodge, even as the chief's three wives, all sisters, ran outside to gossip with the new arrivals.

There was a ceremony to be performed, and the old man sat calmly as it began. In his youth he had been impatient and eager to exchange news. Now he liked this. He liked sitting with someone a while before saying anything. And with Faith and the others fresh upon his mind, he preferred to say little.

From a soft pouch made of the skin of an unborn buffalo calf, the chief removed his medicine pipe, emblem of his office. Its bowl was red pipestone, quarried not far away, and a long slender stem had been fashioned from some hardwood that Lamb did not recognize. Quietly the chief tamped fresh and choice tobacco into it and lit it with an ember. Then, solemnly, he saluted the cardinal directions, the sky, and Mother Earth, and then handed it to Lamb, who puffed slowly and returned it to the chief. They did not talk until the charge of tobacco had been burned and the pipe was returned to its pouch. Richard Lamb was at ease. Sunshine drove through the translucent cowhide lodge-cover, providing a gentle and comfortable light on a glaring summer day.

"Have you come for a visit with the People?" asked Little Plume. "There are some still on the reservation, but most of us are here, and all our bands are here: the Hard Top Knots, the Small Brittle Fat, the Black Patched Moccasins, the Never Laughs, the Quarrelers, the Grease Melters, the Buffalo Dung, the Lone Eaters, the Black Door, and yes, your own Small Robes."

"No, we were forced here by the soldiers from Fort Shaw."

Little Plume frowned.

"Because of the troubles with the Sioux and Cheyenne, the star chiefs ordered all Indians to their reservations."

The chief pondered that. "We have not heard of this thing," he said. "We left upon our summer hunt as usual, and with the blessing of the ninnana —the Agent. But tell me, Lamb, where is your lovely Aspen?"

Lamb sighed. "She and her brother Black Wolf were detained by the soldiers at my post. She is well and I will bring her here soon. Or the soldiers will."

"There was trouble?" asked the chief, his dark eyes intent upon the trader.

"Ye could call it that," Lamb said. "A rash young captain—a subchief—took offense."

"Do you bring this trouble here?"

"Not at all. When the soldiers saw we were coming north, to the reservation, they returned to

Fort Shaw. We are glad to be here. But it has been a hard and sad journey."

He told the chief about Faith and her child and the grandparents.

The chief sat silently. "I knew all was not well," he said eventually. "You are travelling very light, without lodges, without travois, and your horses are weary."

"Our possessions are cached in the Crazy Mountains and the lodges stand at my post. We will return to them when we can."

"Stay here. I have never seen the buffalo so thick. The valley to the east is black with them. Our young men shoot many and would shoot more but we have been denied cartridge ammunition for our Henrys and Winchesters, and we must use our old flintlocks. Why is that, do you know?"

"Yes," said Lamb. "The president—the Great Father in Washington—forbade the sale of metal cartridges to Indians after the defeat of Custer last summer. I have many with me and will share them with ye'r hunters."

"That is good. We will all have meat, then. And we, in turn, will give you robes and lodge-skins and fresh meat from the hunt, until you have gained all you have lost."

"That is kind and welcome."

The chief sat silently, pondering what he would say next. "Last summer the Sioux sent runners bearing a twist of tobacco," he said. "We received the runners. They invited us to fight the soldiers after their great victory over Custer. Together, they said, we shall drive away the napikwan forever. We consulted, and the Blackfeet federation declined. The Piegan declined. The Siksika declined, and the Blood, up in the land of the Great Queen Mother, declined as well. The runners were very angry and threatened us. But we are glad. Life continues peacefully. We are rich with buffalo. Our lands stretch as far as we can see."

Lamb refrained from replying. He wanted to say to Little Plume that things weren't as good as that; that the buffalo would soon be gone and the lands they roamed would most likely be taken away, piece by piece.

"The Agent did not hold ye to the reservation?" Lamb asked. "He blessed this hunt? Ye had no word from the generals, the star chiefs, to stay near the Agency?"

"None," said Little Plume. "The annuity goods from the Great Father did not come this year, so the Agent was eager for us to hunt and feed ourselves with buffalo. He was glad that we went out."

For nothing, then, Lamb thought. For nothing had he suffered, had his daughter and in-laws died. It had been an army stupidity, men with guns blundering into his life, his home, his livelihood.

Even as Lamb and the chief exchanged news

235

and talked for a half hour more, an inner resolve grew in him.

He would leave his kin here. They would be safe in the lodges of their relatives, where they could eat well, prepare robes and lodge-skins, and join the hunt. He would not take them to the agency. He would, instead, ride alone to Fort Shaw and have it out with the army. He had never met Colonel Ambrose, but he intended to meet him, and to talk, and talk, and talk.

At his age, he felt his powers of persuasion were the only real weapons he had left.

# CHAPTER 16

That afternoon, White Buffalo Skull Woman, eldest wife of Chief Little Plume, washed and mended Richard Lamb's trail-grimed buckskins until they shone golden again, and all the sacred-symbol beadwork was as good as Aspen had made it. Lamb bathed and washed his hair in the creek, and when his hair dried it made a great white halo around his face.

At daybreak he set off alone for Fort Shaw, riding the spotted white medicine stallion that had been curried by his grandson Luke Old Coyote until it shone. The fort was forty miles west across flat prairie, a long day's ride. Lamb found a gleaming Henry in his saddle sheath—

Turtle's, no doubt. And his kit had been miraculously replenished with jerky and sarvis-berry pemmican and a chunk of freshly cooked buffalo tongue. He had insisted on going alone. Hope and Turtle had acquiesced solemnly, as was proper for them to do. But his daughter's face was etched with worry.

It was an uneventful trip that consumed the summer day. When the sun was long and golden he rode into the fort, with light splintering and shattering off of him, and illumining his white hair as it danced in the breezes. It was a large place, a quadrangle without a stockade, manned by four companies of cavalry, plus mounted and unmounted infantry. He rode the dancing stallion to a verandahed headquarters building where guidons and an American flag waved. This was a mortared fieldstone structure. The rest of the post was built of logs.

At the tie-rail were several drooping and dusty horses, recently used, bearing the US brand. Around the verandah were yellow-chevroned troopers who did not seem to be at home in this place, and were waiting for something.

He dismounted stiffly. "Could ye tell me where I'd find Glenn Ambrose?" he asked the nearest man.

"Inside, Sir, I believe. We're here from Ellis."

There was no foyer. He stepped into a white-washed, spartan room where two blueclad officers talked across a rough desk. One of the officers, the one covered with trail dust, he knew.

"Barney Beeman," he exclaimed. "I never thought to find ye here."

The response of these two men was strange, he thought. Recoil, astonishment, uneasiness, and then Colonel Beeman's false and crackling cheer. The man's mouth smiled but the eyes were darkly somber. He was introduced to the commander and invited to sit.

"I arrived a few hours ago, and well, we've been talking about you, Lamb," Beeman said gently.

There was a deepening malaise in Lamb's soul now, and his senses keened to trouble.

Ambrose eyed Beeman and seemed to remove himself from whatever was to come.

"There's a young captain here who's laid all sorts of accusations upon you . . . ," Barney Beeman began softly.

"That's what I rode here to talk to ye about."

"These . . . accusations don't seem to fit with what I know of you, or what—I saw at your post."

"Ye went to my post?" he said slowly.

"I did. In response to the dispatch Captain Partridge sent."

"And ye got a mixed-up story ye'r still sorting out. I'll tell ye my version of it when ye'r ready."

"Well, no, Lamb. There was no one at the trading post to talk to."

Colonel Beeman's eyes had grown moist and

soft, and the old man didn't like the feeling in his bones.

"Aspen wasn't there?"

"She's dead, Lamb."

He didn't want to believe what he had just heard. Not Aspen. He started to stand, and then sat down again.

"And so is Black Wolf."

The old man stared bleakly at his friend.

"Aspen was shot—executed, in fact—by Captain Partridge." Beeman's voice cracked. "Her brother died . . . inside the burning post after he killed two troopers and injured three more."

"Ye'd better tell me about it," said Lamb.

Beeman and Ambrose did it step by step. And the story they told the old trader was one they had pieced together from Beeman's careful examination, and from what they had been able to worm out of Murphy, Rudeen, and the other soldiers. Then they told him Partridge's version, and how greatly at odds it was with the evidence that Beeman and Ambrose had pulled together.

There was one thing that Beeman said nothing about; it would only add intolerable pain to the old man's grief—the severing of Aspen's head.

"She was a great lady, and I buried her as one," Barney Beeman said. "We wrapped her in a shroud and I led the men in a prayer. We fired a three-volley salute. I had the men burn her name in a plank. It says Aspen Lamb. . . . Maybe you'll want to make a stone, with the dates, later. I loved her, Lamb . . . there was no one like Aspen. . . ."

The colonel turned a wet-cheeked face to the window and continued, "There was . . . little of Black Wolf to bury, but we made a place for him, near her."

"On the trip north," Lamb said quietly, "we had a hard crossing. I lost my daughter Faith, and a grandchild, Laughing Girl. And both Aspen's parents. And now Aspen and Black Wolf—all for nothing."

Neither officer could talk.

"There's things ye haven't told me yet," he added.

"That's the whole story, Lamb, everything we know," said Glenn Ambrose. "I'm sorry—I'm so sorry."

"What are ye going to do with this Captain Partridge? This man that murdered Aspen. And his brother? These brothers that have put five deaths upon me?"

"We were discussing that very thing when—you walked in," said Beeman.

"And what'll ye be doing about my post? My goods? My livestock? And what'll ye be doing about those soldiers that devil charged with mutiny because they would not murder my wife? Bring charges and court-martial against those boys?"

"They'll escape lightly, I'm sure," said Ambrose.

"Escape lightly? They're men to shake hands

with, those soldiers. Not the officers in ye'r god-damned army." He glared at them. "I left my people with Little Plume, out hunting buffalo. Little Plume knew nothing of any army order keeping them on the reservation. Nothing! The Agent blessed their hunt—get ye'r buff, he said. So where did this order come from and why was it aimed at me?"

Ambrose sighed. "It came a month or so ago by wire. I knew of no Piegan off the reservation, and didn't think the order would apply to your kin, so I did nothing. It was Partridge's idea. He approached me. He and his brother said there were Piegan down there that should be herded north, and he'd go get them. I agreed. I had the order, and the captain seemed eager to enforce it. So . . . I sent him off."

Beeman stared. "I didn't know it had been entirely Partridge's initiative," he said.

"I can see now it was probably some sort of glory trip," said Ambrose dourly.

There was a long silence.

"Little Plume's worried you're going to come after him," said Lamb, "and stop the buffalo hunt and run them back to the reservation. The buff are all they've got to eat. No annuity goods. Teamsters won't come through here after the Little Big Horn. The buff are all the Piegan have."

The CO twisted his waxed mustache. "How long will it take them? The hunt, I mean."

241

"Two, three more weeks."

"Maybe in three weeks we'll check out some rumors that the Piegan are off the reservation."

"It was all for nothing," said Lamb.

"I agree with you, Lamb," Beeman said quietly, "and I will personally begin court-martial proceedings against Partridge. It won't be easy. Not cut-and-dried."

"You'll have my support," said Ambrose.

"Why won't it be easy?" demanded Lamb.

"Because Aspen was an Indian. And they will say a hostile. And you know what some people's idea of a 'good Indian' is as well as I do."

"Lot of good ye'r proceedings'll do," muttered Lamb.

"You must be tired, Lamb. It's getting dark. I'll get an orderly—you've the hospitality of the fort. We'll get your mess, and a bunk. Grain your horse . . . talk more in the morning. Lots more to talk about. There's a chapel here if you want to go—"

"No." Lamb rose. "Thank you."

He stared at one, and then the other, with his wet blue eye. He was tired. He stumbled stiffly to Colonel Beeman, hugged him briefly, and then walked out. He paused on the verandah in the soft summer twilight. Lamplight yellowed the barracks windows and cast long shadows across the parade ground. The northern sky was violet, shading to indigo. He tightened the cinch on his medicine stallion and unwrapped the reins from the hitch-rail.

Someone was staring at him.

"It's you!" shouted Captain Partridge. "You're under arrest, Lamb. This time you won't get away. Soldier!"—he pointed at a trooper—"Hold this man."

Captain Partridge pawed at his holster and yanked out his revolver.

Richard Lamb was weary and he didn't much care what happened. The trooper approached. Partridge waved the revolver. Lamb slid the shining brass-framed Henry from its beaded sheath, not to shoot with, but as a club. The arcing stock caught Joseph Partridge broadside across the face. The powerful blow mashed his ear, broke his jaw in three places, knocked out all but two teeth on the left side of his mouth, and ripped a gash on his face. As he tumbled, Joseph Partridge squeezed the trigger once, twice, five times. The shots all went wild. One barely missed his gawking brother Peter.

"Stop him," slurred the captain from his bloodied mouth. The trooper approached.

The door swung open, spilling lamplight upon the verandah and the ground beyond, and in the doorway loomed the bulky figure of Barney Beeman, taking it all in. He watched Lamb climb up on his white stallion and glide the Henry back into its sheath, saw Partridge rolling in agony on the ground, the revolver in the dust and the smell of gunpower in the air. Saw Lamb quietly touch heels to the horse and rein it away.

"Let him go," said Colonel Beeman. Several troopers who were coming to help, froze. "Let Richard Lamb go," said the colonel. Ambrose appeared on the verandah behind him and nodded. They watched the trader on the spotted horse ride past the barracks, yellow light and black shadow alternating across the flanks of the horse.

"Take the captain to surgery, easy now," Ambrose said. "Post a guard there, he's confined to quarters."

"For what?" shouted Peter Partridge.

"Mr. Partridge," said Glenn Ambrose, "following mess in the morning, you will be escorted to Fort Benton. Your escort will be instructed to detain you in a room there until the next river packet leaves for the East. You will be on that steamer."

"It's an outrage," shouted Peter. "When I get back there I'll have your head. I'll write—"

"Do that," said Barney Beeman, who had been watching.

Richard Lamb rode out into the night. There was still a long streak of blue on the horizon to light the way.

All for nothing, he thought.

He did not know which way to ride, and it was a strangely hard decision. Not south, back to the post which was now a pile of ash with the graves of his wife and brother-in-law that he couldn't bear to look at.

He might go west, to the mountains. In fact, he knew he would go there eventually. But now he would go east, back to Little Plume's people. He had lost Faith, but he still had Hope. His kin would welcome him, heal him, come sit beside him in vigil, saying nothing, letting their presence say everything. He had news for them; sad news.

As he rode, an idea began to take shape in his mind. Something he wanted, something that would delight his soul for whatever years remained. The more he thought of it, the gladder he became. He made camp in a shallow coulee a few miles from the fort. Some spring runoff was still pooled in it and there was willow brush for wood.

The next afternoon he was drenched by a sudden shower that chilled his golden buckskins. There was no refuge. He dismounted and walked, letting the work of his old body warm him. By late afternoon he had reached the great Piegan camp and trotted on down the long slope. Hope and her children, the widower Standing Bear, the motherless Bigtooth Beaver, and nine-year-old Pawing Horse, were there. Turtle was off on a hunt with a borrowed buffalo runner and the old carbine.

There were no preliminaries. "Hope," he began, "your mother is dead. And your uncle." Then he switched to the Blackfeet tongue so the others might understand. He told the story harshly and without detail. Hope's eyes glistened and her face was long but other than that she showed no feeling—for now. In Blackfeet life there was always a time, a season, for grief.

Richard Lamb was glad to be here. He had come to feel more at home among these people than among his own kind. At Fort Shaw he had been an alien. Now, over half a century since he had left white civilization behind, he was as much a Blackfeet as these bronze people around him.

They offered him buffalo hump but he was not hungry. He went, instead, to the great high lodge of Little Plume to pay his respects. He was welcomed, and once again, the medicine pipe was smoked silently.

Then he repeated his story. The eyes of the raw-boned chief flooded with sorrow. He had known Aspen and had fought fights and stolen many horses beside Black Wolf.

"Four days I will stay in my lodge to mourn," he said. Four was the sacred number of the Piegan.

"I am honored."

Then a more practical thing. "Will the soldiers come?" asked little Plume. "Will they stop the hunt and force us back?"

Lamb could not be sure what the U.S. Army would do. Finally he said, "Ambrose asked how long the hunt might last. I told him another three weeks—almost a moon. He said that perhaps after that time he would come to see about rumors that the Piegan were off the reservation."

The chief was not pleased. "We are herded by these men like cattle. The treaty goods never came and now they wish to stop the hunt. Is it that they wish to starve us to death?"

"That's the design of some, not all, yes," said Lamb.

"I will mark days," Little Plume said. "For twenty days we will hunt. On the twenty-first we will go. Now then, Trader Lamb, what are you going to do? You are always welcome among us."

Richard Lamb told him the plan he had, the one that had brought him joy last night. The chief's brown eyes softened. "It is good," Little Plume said. "It is a good thing for an old man. We will be close by. Your daughter, Tall Grass Bending, will visit you often with her children."

Richard Lamb left the chief and strode among the lodges seeking Standing Bear and a permission. His son-in-law was not among the lodges but off alone, out among the horses. He had only one horse now, and no buffalo runner, and he had suddenly become poor. Lamb found him brooding, and began to talk quietly in the Blackfeet tongue.

"There's enough left in my accounts so that you and Turtle will each have Winchester repeaters and good buffalo runners and whatever ye shall need here," he began. Then he got the permission he sought. Standing Bear smiled.

He found Hope and her children, and more importantly, Bigtooth Beaver and Pawing Horse there. He beckoned to Hope to come listen and then drew Faith's adolescent son and slim daughter to him. He spoke to them in English.

"I'd like ye to come live with me and be my family, young man and young lady. What would ye think of that, eh?" He didn't wait for an answer. "I'll teach ye the Blackfeet things, for I know them as well as ye'r grandmother Aspen. And I'll teach ye the white man things, for ye have my blood too. Ye'll listen to my stories about long-time-ago people called Greeks and Romans. And ye'll learn to read words and write and do figures. And we'll run a few cattle and ye'll care for them. And I'll make sure ye are at home in this world that is coming. And ye'll have lots of company, with Aunt Hope here, and the cousins and kin all visiting. And ye'd make an old grandfather happy, ye would, blessing his home."

Faith's children nodded, bright-eyed, and it was settled.

Richard Lamb stayed for the rest of the hunt, walking out each sunny day upon the high plains, letting go of Aspen. It was hard to let go. But after a while he could remember her and smile. And smile too at the thought of Faith, and the others.

Then, as the heavily-laden procession of the Piegan trekked north, Lamb and his young family, and a dozen young men, including Turtle and Standing Bear, rode to a place in the foothills of the Rockies where the Teton River was small and cold, the grass was good, and there was shelter from the Cold Maker's winds. And there, with axes, they felled lodgepole and peeled it and built a fine log home and a shed and a barn and a corral, even as the old man directed. Others came, bringing buffalo robes and fine skins and blanket capotes and various gifts. From Little Plume came ten fine horses and a parfleche of pemmican. And when it was done they celebrated with a brief dance, and left. Bigtooth Beaver, Pawing Horse, and Richard Lamb watched them go on down the river.

"Go pick out ye'r horses, ye two, and ye can begin the breaking of them, Bigtooth Beaver," he said. "And then when ye grow weary of that, come here to this porch and I'll tell ye about a brave man, who lived across the waters long ago, and whose name was Caesar."

# EPILOGUE

The portly man with eyes the color of new ice and a voice with a century of cultivation behind it was a good host. The banquet of Chesapeake Bay crabs had gone famously. The Albany patrician and philanthropist then handed the keys to this fine federal-period building five blocks from the White House to General-of-the-Army William Tecumseh Sherman. The place was, he said, ever more to be an officers' club, a small gift to the men who had led the nation's armies. Sherman accepted the keys. The lesser, but very senior, officers present cheered.

Sherman did not know, but a few of his juniors did, that there was a small quid pro quo. But it was nothing, really. It had to do with the alleged shooting of a squaw, a hostile one at that. Just why Barney Beeman had made such a fuss about it at the brink of retirement, and why Ambrose had backed him, was beyond the understanding of sensible men. But it was nothing. Now Beeman was gone, retired. And Ambrose they had packed off to Arizona to keep an eye on the Chiricahua Apaches.

The very day that the new man had arrived to take over Fort Shaw certain files had disappeared—burned actually—and a young captain ceased to worry about his future. At least his military future. His personal life would always remain difficult, thanks to the grotesque ruin of his face.

In New York, a young, womanizing voluptuary who wrote news stories, but lived much higher than any reporter could afford, was secretly grateful to Barney Beeman for not sending those dispatches he'd written. The stories had been brash and so far from reality that their publication would have put him in very hot water. But thanks to his captivity with the old renegade—a story he told and retold with embellishments to the ladies he squired—he was able to write with more savvy, and a veneer of truth.

The published stories were more careful but no less lurid. And for a while New York readers—and the rest of the nation—were bemused by pieces about an old one-eyed renegade who fed arms to Indians and had no doubt contributed to the Custer debacle, who had the soul of a pirate, and who was a corruptor of the people of the red race. What's more, this renegade had injured a brave young officer, but found strange backing in certain army circles that seemed eager to protect the rascal, rather than bring the old pirate to justice.

The protagonist of all these stories was blissfully unaware of them, and if he had known of them it wouldn't have mattered. He was indifferent to the opinions of the eastern world. Even so, Peter Partridge, in his mind's eye, saw the old pirate quaking in terror from what Partridge had written.

Barney Beeman settled in the Gallatin valley, not far from Fort Ellis. He had come to love that prospect and had stayed. He did see the stories, saw himself pilloried, and laughed. He was out and he was free. Still, when he heard that Joseph Partridge had been made a major he was riled. He thought about that some, and decided it was worth the long trip. He turned his ranch over to his Indian segundos and donned his one civilian suit of black worsted and caught a stagecoach south. Several days later he boarded a glossy varnished Pullman sleeping car on the Union Pacific, at Corinne, Utah, and settled into a plush, wine-colored seat. A few days later he was in Washington having a fine lunch with General-of-the-Army "Cump" Sherman.

The general listened to Barney Beeman's story, sorting out details as he always did. Sherman cared nothing about the trader's Indian squaw, but about certain untruths apparently employed by Major—then Captain—Partridge, he cared a good deal. The man was an officer, but not a gentleman. And about the use, abuse, and persecution of certain enlisted men, who had all mustered out now, he was distressed. All these things he summarized in a confidential memorandum, placing a copy of it in Partridge's file. The major was transferred to a dreary quartermaster position at Fort Leavenworth.

But Barney Beeman was not done. He took a train to New York, marched into the offices of the *Herald*, and stunned Peter at his desk. The message was simple and twofold: if there were any further columns and stories, Peter would die young. And if the new major out at Leavenworth attempted to molest the old trader, two Partridges would die young. With that, Beeman caught a Pullman back West. A few weeks later, General Sherman promoted Glenn Ambrose.

Richard Lamb never returned to Elk Creek. He did not wish to subject himself to that, although he was tempted because he wanted to see where Aspen, she who had lain in his arms, was buried. He did not buy a stone for her as other white men might have. Instead, he caused to have planted directly upon her grave a thick, hardy rosebush which immediately prospered and grew into a great thorny thicket a few rods from the creek. And each year thereafter, the rose bush bloomed profusely in late June, and the roses were blood red.

Wind and rain and blowing dust covered the ashes of the old post until grass grew there. Where the cache had been there remained a slight depression, but no one knew that it was the work of man rather than nature. It was a good place, and in 1880, a rancher settled there and in the protected flats, he built lambing sheds for his sheep. And each spring woolly lambs bleated and pounced where the old post had stood.

Richard Lamb lived until the winter of 1884. In that time a great starvation had come upon the Piegan on the reservation. The buffalo were gone and the government proffered so little food that a third of the tribe died. Lamb was not among those who starved. He had his own small cattle herd which his grandchildren nurtured. He died, rather, attempting to drive fifty longhorns from his Teton ranch to the Blackfeet Agency in the dead of winter. He froze to death, but the cattle saved the life of Tall Grass Bending, her children, and many others. They buried Richard Lamb on his ranch at a place that overlooked the river.

**Center Point Large Print**
600 Brooks Road / PO Box 1
Thorndike, ME 04986-0001 USA

(207) 568-3717

US & Canada:
1 800 929-9108
www.centerpointlargeprint.com